His Christmas Rose

Jane Maguire

His Christmas Rose

Copyright © 2024 Jane Maguire

Cover design by Holly Perret

ISBN: 978-1-7382727-4-7

www.janemaguireauthor.com

Also by Jane Maguire

His Christmas Rose

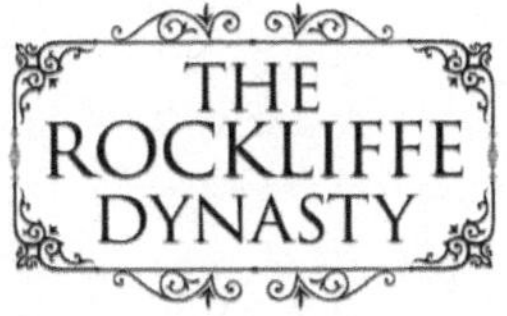

By Jane Maguire

1

December 23, 1816

Lady Emily Prescott couldn't say for sure what aspect of the cacophony caused her last thread of composure to snap. Was it her stepsister Anna and cousin Alexander loudly arguing about which yuletide treat reigned supreme? (Mince pies, Anna insisted, while Alexander remained adamant that the honor belonged to Christmas pudding.) Was it her two younger cousins pounding out a duet on the pianoforte, faintly resembling God Rest Ye Merry Gentlemen, while the girls' three-year-old brother sang another tune altogether? Perhaps it was the noise of her grandmother's bell, the relentless *ting-a-ling* alerting the servants that, yet again, the dowager marchioness required something.

Whatever the case, Emily threw down the wreath she'd been fashioning, letting out a sound that could in no way be considered ladylike. A sound that, really, should have held no ability to compete with the uproar in the Beaumont Manor drawing room. Nonetheless, the argument stopped. The bell ceased ringing. The pianoforte music faded away. Only little James continued his song, stomping his feet against the floor to help him keep tempo. All other eyes, though, were on Emily.

"Is something the matter, Em?" Her father, who'd ensconced himself on the settee in the far corner with her step-mother at his side, was the first to speak, breaking away from their quiet conversation to cast her a curious look.

"It's ..." She frowned, the greenery she'd tossed onto the end table and the pile of adornments surrounding it beginning to swim before her eyes. "This wreath is all wrong. The ribbons aren't cheerful enough. And the berries are too ... too *red*."

Red, just like the color her cheeks started turning. The weight of so many gazes bore into her, and she knew she sounded ridiculous. She was becoming incensed by a bunch of holly branches, for heaven's sake, a festive decoration that should have brought her joy but instead had gone awry.

"What's wrong, Papa, is that she's heartsick," Anna supplied—*not* helpfully. "She'll cheer up once her beau arrives."

"It's not that!" Emily glowered at her sister, knowing she sounded waspish but unable to help herself.

From across the room, her eldest cousin, Benedict—of an age with herself and similarly quiet-natured—looked up from his book to shoot her a sympathetic look. In turn, Alexander winked at her before distracting Anna with another rejoinder about Christmas pudding. Which perhaps should have made Emily feel better, but her face only burned hotter instead. Her mood had nothing to do with Lord Coleville, who was set to arrive at Beaumont before nightfall and would stay with them until the new year.

But nor could she truly attribute her short temper to some displeasing berries, could she?

"Emily?" Her stepmother, Phoebe, rose from the settee, giving her husband a squeeze upon the shoulder before approaching Emily's armchair. "I have something to see to in the kitchen and could use your assistance. Join me?"

Emily could hardly stand fast enough. With a final loathing glance at her discarded wreath, she accepted Phoebe's proffered arm, following the rhythm of her stepmother's foot-falls as they exited the drawing room without another word.

Not that she held any illusions about appearing dignified.

Fortunately, the corridor was indeed much calmer, pulling her away from the recommencement of piano music and a mince pie argument. The empty space proved less stifling, too, giving her face a chance to cool before they encountered a renewed blast of heat in the kitchen.

At once, she was hit with the welcoming fragrance of cinnamon and cloves, and while she couldn't claim the area was peaceful, the kitchen maids' flurry of activity and low chatter as they worked proved far more of a soothing hum than what she'd left behind in the drawing room.

Emily inhaled deeply, taking stock of the large worktable where trays of confectionary drops had been laid out, along with a steaming gingerbread cake. Later, she would take great delight in sampling the confections—her family liked to poke gentle fun at her sweet tooth. For now, though, she turned to Phoebe, concentrating on the task at hand. "Is there some problem with the menus?"

"None whatsoever." Phoebe steered her toward the work-table and released her arm, flashing her a small grin. "There is, however, freshly baked gingerbread in urgent need of sampling."

Emily's brows lifted, and she didn't know whether to smile or frown. Her stepmother didn't require assistance in the kitchen; Phoebe was humoring her.

Yet that was because, after displaying an outburst far too

juvenile for a woman of three-and-twenty, Emily *warranted* humoring.

With a sigh, she let her elbows droop onto the wooden surface, her stomach a strange tangle of knots. However, when the cook, Mrs. Hodges, rushed over with a serving knife, cutting off a thick slice of the cake and holding it out to her, Emily didn't turn it down.

"Thank you." She nodded her appreciation to the cook, taking her first small bite and savoring the mixture of sweetness and spices that burst over her tongue. The flavor was comforting, reminiscent of Christmas seasons past when all that existed was joy and she *hadn't* found herself so irritable.

Beside her, Phoebe nibbled at her own piece of gingerbread, refraining from conversation just as she had in the corridor. Instead, they ate in companionable silence with only the whir of kitchen noise in the background, until the warm, spongy cake filled her, the thought of wreaths no longer stoked her ire, and a quiet *thank you* crossed her lips again, this time directed at her stepmother. The woman who, without a word, had determined exactly what Emily needed.

Phoebe brushed a few crumbs from her fingers before giving Emily's arm a reassuring pat. "It does get a little overwhelming with everyone about, doesn't it?"

"Mm." Emily glanced toward the ceiling where, as if on cue, something crashed against the floor above.

There was no denying that the house had become chaotic over the past few days. But at the same time, she didn't wish any part of it away. She adored her family and so seldom got to see her cousins all under the same roof. They'd been drawn together unexpectedly this month by the family matriarch, the Dowager Marchioness of Rockliffe, whose development of a lung inflammation and fever the week before St. Thomas's Day had left everyone fearing the worst. However, no sooner did the dowager's extended family arrive at Beaumont than the resilient old lady—whom Emily's father, the marquess, often likened to a fire-breathing dragon when he thought his daughters weren't listening—came out of her ague, and her cough began to dissipate. The fact that the visitors planned to remain with them until after Christmas Day, just to ensure the dowager didn't suffer a relapse—which was looking increasingly unlikely, given her ability to relocate to the drawing room and utter demands with such vigor—was a gift. Albeit a very noisy one. Add to that Lord Coleville's imminent arrival and it should truly be the perfect Christmas.

Why, then, was the warmth in Emily's belly dissipating already, leaving behind another wave of that strange churning sensation? The one that had been growing all month, putting her on edge and making her feel like she could scream at the top of her lungs.

She pushed herself up from the worktable, peering toward the row of windows that let in the afternoon's muted gray light. "Perhaps I'd benefit from a walk."

Phoebe nodded. "Yes, I'm sure that would do you good. Shall I join you? I need to check with Mrs. Connelly about how the St. Stephen's Day boxes are coming along, but after that—"

"Thank you, but there's no need." Once again, Emily experienced a swell of gratitude for her stepmother's thoughtfulness. Even when Phoebe's tasks as marchioness and hostess pulled her in a dozen different directions, she didn't hesitate to offer companionship. However, Emily would prove poor company, and she may as well be honest. "I think I require some time alone."

Fortunately, Phoebe understood and made no efforts to dissuade her. She simply waited alongside her as a maid fetched Emily's winter apparel, and once Emily was clad in her cloak and half-boots, Phoebe accompanied her to the kitchen door.

"Take as much time as you need, as long as you're certain to return home by dark." She gave another of her gentle, encouraging smiles before pulling the latch and opening the door to the winter landscape beyond. "Oh, and Emily? If you feel inclined to try your hand again at wreath-making, I noticed the holly was in abundance at the east side of the estate, bordering the stream."

The stream. An icy prickle shot down Emily's spine, and not from the sudden blast of cold air. The stream delineated the border between Beaumont and Rosemead, the neighboring estate. A place she'd visited often as a child; in fact, Viscount Pembrook of Rosemead had made it a tradition to invite Lord Rockliffe and his family for dinner every year on Christmas Eve. Of course, for the past seven years, Emily had invented excuses not to attend. A megrim. Fatigue. A stomachache. Her inevitable string of illnesses—always on Christmas Eve and gone the next morning—no doubt caused a few eyebrows to rise, although no one had ever prodded her about it too thoroughly.

But what difference did any of that make now? The long-standing tradition was to be broken this year, for Lord Pembrook had been on the Continent since the summer, and his son—*Nate*—had apparently traveled there to join him for the yuletide season.

As a result, Rosemead House was closed up indefinitely. Its occupants far away. There was absolutely no reason she shouldn't venture near Beaumont's easternmost boundary.

She stiffened her shoulders, then uttered farewell to Phoebe and stepped out onto the frosty grass. Light snow had begun drifting down from the sky, and although the day was chilly and dull, it also held a sort of stark beauty. The perfect backdrop against which to clear one's head.

Only when she'd crossed the expansive back lawn, gone over the footbridge, and started venturing into the woods did it occur to her that she should have remained at the house so she wouldn't risk missing Lord Coleville's arrival.

And furthermore, Phoebe hadn't said a word about him.

2

His return to England had unquestionably been a mistake.

Nathaniel Pembrook tugged the ropes encircling the hefty ash log, and still, the recalcitrant thing wouldn't budge. He should have brought the sled. Should have brought a footman or sought out a few boys from the village. Better yet, he should have stayed in France.

But he *hadn't* done that, he inwardly grumbled as he took a step back and planted his feet against the frosty ground, wrapping the ropes a little more tightly around his one functional hand. No, he'd arrived back at Rosemead right on time for the festive season. Which was a bloody—*tug*—stupid—*tug*—mistake.

He'd managed well enough to locate a small tree trunk that could act as a yule log, fell it, and even secure it with a few adequate knots. However, somewhere along the way, the log had shifted into a mud puddle that hadn't yet frozen, and he'd be damned if he could get it back out.

The sensible action, of course, would be to neglect it as a lost cause and return to the house to seek help. Yet his decisions of late were proving decidedly senseless, and he desired few things less than disturbing the few overworked staff members who remained at Rosemead. Plus, the sky had taken on an ominous gray tinge, the few flakes of falling snow seeming to hint at weather far more severe.

He was going to do this now. Alone. If he just pulled the ropes a *little ... harder ...*

His body lurched forward, and his arms shot out in a desperate attempt to regain balance, helping him narrowly avoid a collision between the snow-dusted dirt and his face.

"Goddamn it!" The curse flew from his lips as he regained his footing, the echo of it floating up through the trees and mingling with the bucolic sound of birdsong. Yes, he'd remained upright. Hadn't tumbled over his own feet or broken a bone. But likewise, the intended yule log remained wedged in the mud. As if it *knew* he planned to light it on fire and had decided to retaliate.

At what point did his determination become stupidity? At what point did he forsake the venture and admit defeat?

Were he to do so now, no one would know what an ass he'd made of himself aside from the wrens and waxwings above. He could still bring home the pile of holly branches he'd collected, which was something, at any rate—even if the deserted ash trunk would grate at his nerves for the rest of the day. The rest of the yuletide season, more like.

He turned to the holly with another muttered oath, a peculiar twinge shooting across his nape. It was as if the birds had taken to staring at his folly, for he had the distinct sense of being watched.

Which was absurd. Nonetheless, the feeling continued to prick his skin, and when a gentle wind rustled through the woods, making branches quiver, he whirled around abruptly—

Only to be met with two wide, startled eyes. A woman's

eyes, rich and warm like the color of brandy. A woman whose billowing cloak and snowflake-speckled dark hair put him in mind of a winter queen from a fairy story.

A woman whose features were unquestionably familiar.

"Emily." He uttered the name that had long been known to him, although it suddenly felt strange on his tongue. Perhaps because when he'd last uttered it, the name had belonged to a girl. *Lady Emily Prescott,* daughter of the Marquess of Rockliffe, who inhabited the neighboring estate.

Well, that girl had since grown up, her face a striking combination of sharp cheekbones and lush lips. But whereas the girl had used to skip about with her younger sister and offer up shy smiles, the woman stood motionless, as if she were made of stone.

Had she been lingering there, alongside a holly shrub next to the stream, long enough to witness his incompetency and have her ears defiled by his expletive? Or perhaps, as a lady grown, she took offense to his neglecting her title. Regretfully —*very* regretfully—he could do nothing to erase the former. As for the latter, though ...

He straightened his spine, dipping his chin in as dignified a nod as he could muster. "That is, good day, Lady Emily. How nice to see you again."

The expression of horrified shock faded from her eyes, although the look that followed could never be mistaken for pleasure. "Mr. Pembrook. I didn't realize you were returning to England for Christmas." She said it coolly, as if the revelation weren't a welcome one.

"Nor did I." The rejoinder slipped out before he could stop it. *Stupid.* The last thing he needed was to enter a discussion about his poorly executed plan and the weak moment of excessive sentimentality that had prompted it. He brushed a few snowflakes off the sleeve of his greatcoat, trying to appear nonchalant. "It was a spur-of-the-moment decision."

She paused, her brows giving the faintest twitch as she considered his vague explanation. Ultimately, though, only a simple question followed. "Has your father returned as well?"

His father. The man who'd hosted a prolific St. Stephen's Day party for every year of Nate's existence and made it appear easy. "No. He remains in France."

"I see." Her words were so toneless that it was difficult to derive any meaning from them. He nearly imagined a slight dip of her shoulders from beneath her cloak, as if she'd breathed a sigh of relief. However, her face remained flinty; his presence seemed to have that effect on her. "Well, I'll not keep you any longer, Mr. Pembrook. I wish you a happy Christmas."

And then, she spun away with astounding swiftness, her skirts fluttering behind her as she departed the border between their two estates and traipsed deeper onto Rockliffe land.

It occurred to him, after an indeterminate number of seconds passed, that he was both staring and gaping, his eyes following her determined steps and the ebony tendrils that had come loose to trail down her back.

He snapped his jaw closed, executing his own abrupt turn. There was no time to stop and ponder just what he'd done to earn the displeasure of a girl—a woman—he hadn't seen in seven years. There was even less time to think of how her hair looked like strands of silk he very much wanted to stroke, how the frosty air had given her cheeks an alluring flush, how the annoyed little scrunch of her lips as she'd uttered her final words had stirred something in the vicinity of his—

He hastily bent over to sweep the accumulated holly into his arms and make a rapid retreat of his own. Yet as he reached out, a painful spasm shot through his hand, and he staggered, the air flying from his lungs. Which at least made his subsequent curse reside in his head only.

He cradled the injured hand as he waited for the ache to

diminish. This blasted English weather was doing him not a bit of good. The cold seemed to leach to his bones, digging in its icy claws to exacerbate his wound.

Yet England was what he'd chosen. England, with its dreary skies, and its mud puddles, and his father's vacant estate in Kent, and—

And his longtime neighbor, Lady Emily, no longer fleeing but back at his side, her aloofness replaced by wide-eyed concern. "Your hand!" The way she regarded the withered limb—the unsightly yellowish bruising on his skin, the index finger that wouldn't straighten—suggested she hadn't taken notice of his ailment before.

Fortunately, he'd already dispensed with the notion that his dignity remained intact; otherwise, her presence beside him may have come as a blow. He hunched his shoulder, allowing the hand in question to slip a little farther up his sleeve to conceal it. If only his fingers hadn't grown too stiff and painful to cram them inside his glove. "It's nothing," he said. "A souvenir from my travels." A souvenir that had rendered him infuriatingly useless.

"A fracture?"

"Precisely. But I'll live."

Her gaze lingered another moment before she snapped her head upright, quirking a dark brow. "I hope you don't think me too forward by suggesting you should rest your hand and leave the tasks of lifting and carrying to your household staff."

Yes, indeed. He'd do just that, except for the slight problem that his household staff was close to nonexistent. "I'm afraid that's impossible today."

"I see." Again, those words, uttered with such detachment. Yet in the next instant, she shifted, a trace of brightness —or something approaching it, anyway—settling over her features. She took hold of her cloak, her feet getting ready to carry her away. "I'll return to Beaumont Manor, then, and send over a few footmen to assist—"

"No." He spit out the refusal before she'd even finished the last syllable, causing her to halt in her tracks. The birds and Lady Emily had grown privy to his ineptness and humiliation; he had no wish to bring another household's footmen in on it besides. Not to mention, he'd been home less than forty-eight hours and had already imposed on the charity of those at Beaumont. "Thank you," he said with a shred more composure, "but no." *The tattered remains of my pride will not allow it.*

Her eyes narrowed, and while a gust of wind chose that moment to swirl the thickening snowflakes, he also detected the irritated puff of her breath. "Suit yourself. But if your staff cannot assist you today, I hope that means you'll postpone your venture until tomorrow, lest you do yourself further injury upon the boundary of Rockliffe land. Besides, it's bad luck to bring in your greenery prior to Christmas Eve."

He made a sound. A laugh of a sort, although it had a brisk, humorless ring. "Unfortunately, I don't have the time to let luck dictate my actions."

Her brow rose higher, the arch in it suggesting she had questions about his intelligence. "Might I inquire why such urgency?"

"Because, Lady Emily." His voice came out a touch too sharp. Too loud. But suddenly, he couldn't contain it. The snow in his hair was beginning to melt and drip down his neck. His hand hurt like the devil. Everything he'd tried to accomplish since returning to Rosemead was met with yet another damnable obstacle. And she wished to know why the urgency?

"It's a longstanding tradition that the Viscount Pembrook of Rosemead hosts a St. Stephen's Day party as a show of appreciation for his servants and tenants. In my father's absence, I assumed that I, as the future viscount, would be equal to the task." He did laugh at that part, at how idiotically delusional he'd been. "My *urgency* comes from the fact that I've already sent out word the party will go ahead as usual. Even though I have less than three days left to prepare. Even though Rosemead House was supposed to be shut up for the winter, and therefore, most of the servants have already left to spend Christmas with their families. Even though I don't know a damn thing about planning a party, and my right hand is useless, and now, it won't stop bloody snowing!"

He became aware that his breathing had quickened. That his chest had grown tight. That, with the incensed echo of his outburst fading into nothingness, the air surrounding him had become perfectly still. Perhaps he'd frightened off the birds, for not even a single chirp emerged from the trees. As for Emily, her brandy-colored eyes bore into him, although the emotion brewing behind them remained aggravatingly unreadable. Had he stirred a mote of her sympathy? Evoked her ire? Caused her to consider him even more of a numbskull?

He hadn't the faintest idea. Something about those eyes rendered him incapable of thinking straight. All he could do was stare in return, trying to catch his breath, letting the silence linger.

Until suddenly, she was marching away—not abandoning her incompetent neighbor in favor of Beaumont but stepping onto Pembrook land. Her determined footfalls continued until she came to a stop beside his failed attempt at a yule log, her boot shuffling in the layer of newly fallen snow until she uncovered one of the ropes he'd used to secure it.

"What are you doing?" He watched as she leaned down to retrieve it, a subtle sense of unease beginning to pull between his ribs.

"What does it look like?" She straightened, wrapping a

little of the rope around her dainty gloved hand. "If you insist this task needs doing immediately, and you'll accept no offers of help from Beaumont Manor, I see no one here to assist you but me."

"You cannot." He rushed over to her, his mind flashing backward a decade to the thin, pale-faced girl who'd visited Rosemead with her family that Christmastide. Lady Emily had contracted a fever while traveling abroad, one that had nearly cost her her life. One that, even after more Christmases passed, left her quicker to tire and not quite so rosy-cheeked as before.

Well, she certainly didn't appear ill now, although she did remain slender and small of stature. What if she overexerted herself, and it was all on his account? The last thing he needed was to add that to his list of the day's calamities.

He no longer had to guess at her sentiments, for the glower she shot him was downright murderous. She didn't drop the rope; on the contrary, her other hand clamped around a length of it farther down. And then, she pulled, her small body straining forward.

Perhaps unsurprisingly, the yule log didn't move. That didn't stop her from trying again. Her forehead puckered and her face reddened as she tugged, and she was oblivious to—or maybe unconcerned about—the fact that he was standing in front of her, holding up a hand in objection.

He took a rapid step to the side before a collision ensued. "Lady Em—"

"We would succeed much faster if you used your uninjured hand to help instead of standing in the way."

He opened his mouth but then closed it before another protest emerged. Yes, she was small of stature, but he was also beginning to think her capable of doing him bodily harm if he dared tell her again that she *couldn't*.

There was nothing else for it. He grabbed the other rope out of the snow, wrapping it back around his left hand.

"We will count to three and then pull. Yes?" She included the question at the end, although her tone didn't leave any room for refusal. "One, two, *three*."

He scarcely got his bearings in time to comply, although he did manage it, giving a heave just as she finished the count.

The yule log remained stuck in the mud. Of course it did. The thing was going to remain there to taunt him until the end of time, and all he stood to gain by continuing his fruitless attempts was giving Emily a more in-depth view of his struggle.

But she was undeterred. "Again." She readjusted the ropes, allowing him an extra moment this time to follow suit. "One ... two ... *three*!"

Everything happened so fast that he couldn't say what transpired first: the loud squelch behind them, or Emily's sharp gasp as her feet stumbled and her body careened forward.

His own body acted on reflex, dropping the rope like it had scorched him and seizing her before she could fall. Fortunately, she landed in his arms instead of on the ground, and he leaned in to peer at her face, scanning each angle and contour for signs of distress. "Are you hurt?"

For a moment, the world stood still once again. Nothing existed but the vague outline of her curves beneath his fingertips, and rosy lips, and dark lashes adorned by tiny droplets of melted snow.

A moment was all it lasted, though, before she jerked herself free of his grasp and gave her head a little shake, as if she'd never heard anything so foolish. "Of course not. And look, we've done what you set out to achieve. Let's continue."

He'd been so enraptured by her face—her snow-speckled,

flinty-eyed, exertion-flushed, unnervingly striking face—that he hadn't thought to look behind him.

I'll be damned. The sight that greeted him when he turned was none other than the mud-encrusted yule log lying free in the snow.

He cocked his head, peering at the improbable scene. However, his interest in it rapidly waned, his attention turning back to where it truly belonged: upon her. The stubborn slip of a woman who seemed to disdain him but had simultaneously chosen to help solve his dilemma.

Her expression showed no hint of satisfaction or triumph. Rather, her compressed lips and furrowed brow begged a single question of him: *Why are you taking so long?*

He broke the gaze, hurrying over to the pile of holly he'd gathered and using his good hand to tuck it beneath his arm. With that accomplished, he returned to take up the ropes and begin his plodding trek home. Only to find she'd already resumed her position, a rope in hand, ready to keep going.

He bit back another inquiry as to what she was doing— he'd learned his lesson in that regard. Instead, he bowed his head to her, ignoring how the muscles in his neck felt strained. "Thank you, but I won't impose on you further."

She didn't try to conceal her sigh. "If time is of the essence, then this is the fastest way. Not to worry, for I'll go with you only until we come into view of Rosemead House, and your household need never know that you didn't haul it in yourself. I trust you have a footman or groom who can spare the few minutes it will take to bring it as far as your hearth."

"It's not ..." God, she must think him a blunderbuss *and* an ingrate. He *did* appreciate her help. Merely hated the fact he'd needed it in the first place. That he'd gotten so many things wrong. "It's not that," he finished quietly. Dejectedly.

And then, because there was really no other option, he

secured the additional length of rope, and in an unspoken agreement, they began tugging in unison.

Fortunately, the muddy ash log glided over the snow with relative ease, and they traipsed through the woods, the strengthening wind doing them the favor of gusting at their backs.

He chanced to dart a look at her—the flushed cheeks, the increasingly tumbling black locks, the small, cloak-enshrouded body that marched along at a relentless rhythm. Perhaps he should attempt to make conversation. Ask after her family, or if she planned to go to London after the yuletide season. However, her eyes focused straight ahead, as if nothing existed but the woods beyond, and he couldn't imagine she'd welcome his overtures.

He briskly turned his head back, concentrating his attention in kind. Silence it was, then.

Silence, until he detected a barely audible click. Followed by another. And another.

The chattering of teeth.

He peered at her again, letting his eyes linger as unease snaked its way through his gut. But her lips were pinched closed, the noise noticeably absent.

Perhaps it had been a trick of his imagination. A reaction to how the wind had grown so bitter that his body would begin shaking from it if he didn't soon go indoors.

Luckily, they'd nearly made it out of the woods, and the welcome sight of Rosemead would come into view any moment now. The numerous difficulties awaiting him within its walls would almost be worth it for the blazing fire he'd get to enjoy.

Except then, the noise returned. The unmistakable sound of teeth clattering together, and this time, he saw it. She didn't clamp her mouth closed quickly enough to hide how it trembled. To conceal how her lips had turned blue.

He halted abruptly, his gaze traveling up and down her body without remorse. Not unexpectedly, her eyes shot daggers at him, but all of a sudden, that didn't matter in the least. Nothing mattered beyond the sight next to the ground that made him gape.

One of Emily's boots had a hole in the leather. A tear by the side of her foot that must be letting in snow with every step she took.

"What in hell?" He flung down the rope, the branches beneath his arm scattering as he grabbed hold of her, scooping her off the frosty ground and into his arms.

After a split second of shock, her eyes became large and indignant. "What in h-h-hell are *you* doing?" Even though her voice shook from cold, her limbs began flailing against him, trying to break free.

"Oof." A sharp breath escaped him as her elbow connected with his ribs, yet it would take far more than that to dissuade him. He adjusted his arms to obtain a tighter hold on her, feeling his brow knit into a severe vee. "Just how long have you been walking through the snow with a hole in your boot?"

"I s-s-snagged it on a branch. Never mind. You'll do further injury to your hand if you don't put. Me. D-down!"

"*You'll* do further injury to my hand," he bit back, "if you don't cease wriggling. You think I'm going to set you loose and watch as you stagger back into the woods, in this weather, while you could very well be suffering from frostbite? Your chances of that happening are less than those of a snowflake on the sun."

She let out an incensed cry, and he was nearly certain that she released a trace of an obscenity with her next breath. Yet her shivering body no longer fought him. Instead, she rested in his arms as stiff as a board, staring into the distance with the same steely-eyed resolve she'd displayed while dragging in the yule log.

The asinine task he should have insisted harder that she *not* perform. He'd dismissed her postulations about bad luck, although if not luck (or a lack thereof), what else could he label his string of misfortunes? Misfortunes that had now spread to her by association. Be that as it may, he'd be damned if he let her come to harm under his watch.

His hand was useless, but his legs moved faster than ever, breaking through the woods and onto the back edge of Rosemead's manicured gardens, the house appearing like a sanctum in the snow.

Just a little farther and he'd get her indoors, warm. Get her out of his cursed presence so he could sit alone and lament the fact that his afternoon of labor had put him farther behind instead of ahead.

He trudged along, silently damning his idiocy for perhaps the thousandth time that day.

And even so, his brain—or perhaps a lower part of his anatomy—found the capacity to alert him that having her in his arms wasn't an unpleasant sensation in the least.

3

There was a time, many years ago, when Emily would have considered a tryst in Nathaniel Pembrook's arms as her most fanciful daydream come true. His chest was every bit as solid as she'd once imagined it would be. His arms every bit as muscular and supportive. His skin gave off a faint scent she hadn't known would be there, crisp and masculine and thoroughly enticing.

All of which she now considered a nightmare.

She held herself tautly in his embrace, willing her freezing body not to tremble as he burst through the kitchen door of Rosemead House. She would give him no further cause to feel superior.

As it turned out, the kitchen erupted into such a flurry of movement and exclamations that there was no time for him to utter an *I told you so*. Voices intermingled. Chair legs scraped across the floor. And then, she was being dumped upon a wooden seat before the hearth, where, for a moment, the only thing to flood her head was warmth.

The hearty flames were a balm to her ice-cold limbs, and she didn't have the strength to refuse them. The heat seeped into her, making her feel heavy and sluggish, and when Nate knelt on the floor and wrenched off her boots, she didn't even fight him.

Not until it occurred to her, some seconds later, that her foot remained in his palm and he was examining it, peering at the sodden stocking, sending the subtle warmth of his fingertips to the chilled flesh beneath. It felt … soothing. It felt—

She jerked her foot out of his grasp, silently cursing the way her thoughts had strayed. She was in Nate's kitchen, for heaven's sake. Could sense the weight of numerous gazes upon the back of her neck.

She wrenched her head around, taking in the scene behind her. Nate had told her that only the barest staff remained at Rosemead for the yuletide season. Nonetheless, her plight was being observed by a cook and a kitchen maid. A footman in Rosemead's forest green livery. And another wearing familiar royal blue—

"Joseph!" For the first time that day, her mouth curved into a genuine smile, and her tight shoulders sank with relief. She didn't know what a Beaumont footman was doing in the Rosemead kitchen, but nor did she require a reason when his presence meant her salvation. Her escape. "I'm afraid I had a mishap with my boot, but n-no matter. Now, you can take me h-h-home with you."

"No." That dratted Nate loomed beside her, daring to cast a severe look at Joseph before turning it upon her. "For God's sake, Lady Emily, you're still shivering. You can hardly go back into the cold in this state."

Her smile faded as soundly as if it were a lit candle he'd tossed into a snowdrift.

Joseph took a tentative step forward, his brow furrowing uncertainly as he glanced from the vexatious master of the house to the unhelpfully snow-streaked window and then back to her. "I came on horseback, my lady. I'm not sure the weather's fit for you to ride. I suppose I could return to Beaumont and tell the grooms you need the sleigh."

"Yes." She couldn't agree quickly enough. She may very well have jumped up to throw her arms around him if her foot wasn't still numb, and if it wouldn't cause a scene. "Oh, yes, please do."

"There's no need." Again, Nate interjected where he was least wanted, giving the hope she kept trying to drum up another thorough dousing. "*I* will bring Lady Emily home in my sleigh once I've found her some new footwear and she's had a chance to warm up."

Her body betrayed her by shuddering, her teeth clattering together at the very moment she meant to protest.

That was all the convincing Joseph required. "Very good, sir. And not to worry, Lady Emily. I'll tell Lord Rockliffe that you've come to no harm and will be along shortly." He dipped his chin, spinning toward the door before she could utter another word. And Nate, blast him, didn't speak either but followed Joseph without a single backward glance. Leaving her alone to stew.

She shifted beneath her cloak, clamping her arms tightly across her chest as she stared into the flames. Another stretch of minutes in Nate's presence, alone? *Unthinkable.* Yet how could she argue that she was perfectly fit to travel on horseback when her body continued to shake with sporadic tremors? How would she make herself sound anything but immature and petulant?

"Here you are, my lady."

A copper mug appeared before her nose, and she looked up to find the pleasant-faced cook standing over her, holding out the offering. Steam rose from the liquid within, along with an agreeable spiced aroma, effectively vanquishing any thoughts Emily had about refusing it.

Heat spread through her fingertips the moment she

clasped the mug, and a pleasing burn followed when she tipped the drink into her throat. She took several long sips, feeling her muscles grow steadier and a little more of the frostiness melt away. And because Nate was still by the door, engaged in quiet conversation with Joseph, she granted the cook a small smile. "This is lovely. Thank you."

"Certainly, Lady Emily." The older woman beamed in return, two spots of deep pink brightening her cheeks. "It's the least we can do to repay the kindness shown us by everyone at Beaumont Manor today."

Just like that, the comforting warmth turned cold in Emily's belly. "What kindness?" Her fingers tightened around the mug, her nerves pricking with a strange sense of disquiet.

"Why, all this, of course." The cook gestured toward the worktable, which was laden with trays of biscuits, along with several large pies and a plum cake. "When Mr. Pembrook came home and said he'd be holding the St. Stephen's Day party as usual, I told him it couldn't be done. Not with only me and Sally here in the kitchen. But all it took was a note to Beaumont, and next thing, your Mrs. Hodges was sending us over more food than we could have dreamed, all at Lord and Lady Rockliffe's behest. We're that grateful, we are. They're all a true example of what it means to be generous at Christmastide."

Emily remained stock-still, unable even to pretend she returned the cook's cheer. If her parents had instructed that food be sent over to Rosemead, then they knew. Phoebe *knew* Nathaniel Pembrook was in residence when she'd suggested the location for Emily's walk, and she hadn't seen a reason to divulge such pertinent information.

The cook uttered something about needing to check the oven and shuffled away, leaving Emily to slump against the back of her chair and return her gaze to the fire.

If only the truth about Nate returning home had reached

her ears sooner, she never would have gone anywhere near the border between their estates. Then, she wouldn't be trapped in his kitchen in only her stockings. Wouldn't be the girl who bristled at the thought of him believing her incapable. Who bristled even more at how she'd then gone and proved him right.

Her face flamed, the heat no longer welcome but uncomfortable. And yet, this wasn't the most humiliating thing that had ever happened to her at Rosemead House.

As much as she wished it wouldn't, her mind flashed backward to another blazing hearth, just a few stairs and corridors away, upon a long-ago Christmas Eve. It was the year she'd turned thirteen. The year she and her father had returned to England after a lengthy absence, and he'd married Phoebe, and their dear neighbor, Viscount Pembrook, had welcomed the new marchioness by inviting them all for Christmas Eve dinner. The viscount had a beautiful home, warm and bright and elegantly decorated for the season, and the dinner table had been filled with all the delicious food and camaraderie one would want of such an affair.

Except suddenly, none of that had mattered to her. She'd had eyes only for the person sitting directly across the table: Lord Pembrook's son.

She'd always known Nate, of course. However, she'd never truly *seen* him. Never appreciated how his hair curled a little and shone like gold, how his eyes were a stormy shade of gray, how his body had grown long and sculpted and unquestionably male. He *had* become a man, after all, who would soon turn eighteen and transition from Eton to Cambridge. Consequently, her heart had raced and fluttered in a way it had never done before.

She hadn't acted upon her newfound feelings, beyond going home and drawing copious hearts in the pages of her diary. Yet the feelings had stayed with her even as Nate returned to school and winter became spring. They'd stayed throughout each change of season until winter arrived again, and Lord Pembrook repeated the Christmas Eve dinner invitation.

Then, at last, she'd received her reward, for after a full year without their paths crossing, Nathaniel Pembrook had sat across from her once again. Even more dazzlingly handsome than the Christmas before.

She hadn't known how to be charming and flirtatious. His gaze had caused her to blush furiously and stare at her napkin, while she silently willed him just to *know* the depths of her adoration (which hadn't worked).

The following year, though, she'd arrived better prepared. She'd been practicing her smile in the mirror, and when no one was around to hear, she'd accompanied it with a coquettish little laugh.

Unfortunately, her newfound attempts hadn't resulted in a declaration of love on Nate's part; in fact, he'd appeared somewhat grimmer than on Christmases past.

Still, she hadn't been dissuaded. The year after that, she'd donned a new silk frock. Pinched color into her frustratingly pale cheeks. Asked Phoebe's lady's maid to style her hair. Properly adorned, she'd then gone to Rosemead House with a plan. A clever plan, as it had seemed at the time, in which she'd stumble at Nate's feet and he'd immediately come to her rescue. Perhaps he'd even sweep her into his arms, and she'd smile, and her feelings for him would be revealed at last.

As it turned out, Nate had brought a friend home from Cambridge with him that year, and he also looked sullener than ever. Yet she hadn't taken that as reason to change course. She would execute her scheme in the drawing room, she'd decided as they all began strolling there for after-dinner games. When she realized she'd forgotten her shawl upon her chair and would need to pop back to the dining room, she'd viewed it as simply a brief delay.

However, her silent reappearance in the dining room doorway revealed that Nate and his friend hadn't joined the procession to the drawing room after all but remained at the table, wine goblets in hand.

Cheer up, Pembrook, it's Christmastide. The dark-haired young man had given him a lazy smile, clinking the rim of their glasses together. *The drinks are flowing. You have good company and enough food to feed an army. Lord, you even have a pretty little chit to stare at you with stars in her eyes.*

Lady Emily? At once, Nate's head had perked up, although the way he'd uttered her name had been sharp, cheerless. And then, he'd done the worst thing of all. He'd *laughed.* A hollow, dismissive sound that matched the coldness in his eyes. *She's naught but a sickly* child.

Fortunately, she'd had the presence of mind to abandon her shawl and noiselessly race back down the corridor. Even while her heart shattered like a crystal vase flung from the edge of an ocean cliff and onto the jagged rocks below.

She hadn't been lying when she told her father she was unwell and needed to go home early that night.

The lie hadn't come until the following Christmas Eve, when a fictional headache forced her into bed before dinner. Phoebe had made a point of saying that Nathaniel Pembrook was traveling in the Mediterranean and wouldn't be home for the yuletide season. But it hadn't mattered. As much as she esteemed the cordial Lord Pembrook and appreciated his hospitality, Emily couldn't make merry in the same room where Nate had taken her girlish desires and crushed them beneath the sole of his boot.

She couldn't do it that year, nor on any of the Christmas Eves that followed, even though Nate had never returned to England since. Not until today—and only because Lord

Pembrook was also abroad, and there was no chance of receiving a dinner invitation—had she dared to venture anywhere near Rosemead. *And look where that got me.*

Perhaps she was foolish to hold onto petty grievances for so long. After all, time had passed, she'd gone through multiple London Seasons, and she'd reached an age that brought her closer to spinsterhood than girlhood. But even so, she would never forget Nate's words. *She's naught but a sickly child.*

The cold ring of them echoed in her memory, mixing with the cheery pop of flames. Until suddenly, Nate was at her side again, as if her thoughts had conjured him.

She didn't *want* to conjure him. Wanted no more reminders of her silliness and chagrin. Nonetheless, his looming presence remained, and he extended a hand to her. "Will you come with me?"

She jumped up at once—*without* accepting his hand—because he must have deemed her sufficiently warmed. The sleigh would be ready, and she could at last escape to Beaumont and put the misadventure behind her.

Except Nate didn't walk to the door but toward the corridor.

Her stockinged feet froze against the floor. "Where are we going?"

He turned to give her a look that nearly appeared ... *merry.* As if they were old friends, and her visit to his home had been planned and not an unhappy accident. "I want you to see the fruits of your labor."

What on earth was he talking about? She folded her arms across her chest, doing her best imitation of her grandmother's irritated glower.

"It will only take a moment." He went to the doorway and paused, tilting his chin toward the corridor. And then, without waiting to ensure she followed, he departed, leaving behind only the echo of his footfalls.

Drat, drat, drat *him.*

She scurried out of the kitchen, her newly warmed feet flying until they caught up with him near the servant's stairs. He'd promised her a ride home in his sleigh, and she wouldn't let him out of her sight until he made good on that promise. After which she hoped never to see him again.

They climbed the stairs in silence, his footsteps aggravatingly confident and eager. Hers quiet and clipped. She made sure to keep pace with him, lest she be forced to stare at his back.

Why had she let herself feel sympathy for his plight? If she'd returned home on any of the countless occasions he'd tried pushing her away, she would already be back at Beaumont by now, safe from the elements.

Safe from the lingering ache in her heart.

"Here." Nate shoved open a door, and as they stepped over the threshold, they were no longer in a narrow corridor but in Rosemead's great hall. The space, with its soaring ceiling, massive alabaster pillars, and intricate marble work, had always captured her interest when Lord Pembrook guided them through it to reach the dining room.

However, Nate wasn't directing her toward ridged pillars or immaculate carvings, nor toward the haphazard array of tables and chairs that had appeared along the walls. He was peering at the fireplace. Rather, in front of the fireplace, where the muddy piece of tree trunk they'd dragged through the woods had been freed of its ropes and rested upon the floor like a centerpiece.

A peculiar sensation tugged at her chest. Not joy, exactly. Would she go so far as to call it satisfaction? Helping him had cost her both her boots and her dignity. Yet here was proof she'd also accomplished something in the process, that her efforts hadn't all been for naught.

Nate sauntered over to the fireplace, his lips quirking in the suggestion of a grin. She wished she hadn't noticed. Wished she didn't care about his smile, or his injured hand, or his party, or anything to do with the subject of Nathaniel Pembrook. However, it seemed no number of years, no amount of mortification and despair, could render her indifferent.

"Sit on it."

Her body stiffened, the ridiculous words pulling her out of her thoughts. Surely, she'd misheard. But no, he was waiting for her, beckoning to the tree trunk like he presented a gift.

She took a few rigid steps forward, her eyes narrowing. "I beg your pardon?"

"Haven't you heard that the first one to sit upon the yule log before it goes into the fireplace will be favored with good luck?"

She pinched her mouth closed, folding her arms back across her chest. "I thought you didn't have time to believe in luck."

"No." He continued to eye the log, the gray of his irises bright beneath the light of the wall sconces. "But it cannot hurt, can it?"

Was he mocking her? Pacifying her? Did he assume she was too feeble to keep standing?

She's naught but a sickly child.

She pushed the unwanted memory away, surveying him from beneath her lashes. While there were a great many things she could say about Nathaniel Pembrook, nothing in his demeanor hinted at condescension.

She blew out a long breath, crossing the rest of the way to the fireplace. Truth be told, she hadn't placed much credence in luck, either. Not until mere hours ago, when she, too, had brought her greenery indoors early, after which her day had spiraled into a series of calamities wherein each one eclipsed the last.

If there was any chance she could counteract the cloud of misfortune that seemed to be following her, why not take it? She had very little left to lose and everything to gain. And so, she plopped herself down, pulling her spine tall and pressing her palms against the rough bark.

Nothing about sitting on the damp, muddy surface felt particularly lucky. Or dignified.

Yet Nate was peering down at her, his irritating, *wonderful* half-grin growing a notch wider. "Tomorrow, once it has dried out a little, we'll light it."

We ... we'll *light it.* The words sank in, and just like that, all thoughts of smiles and luck vanished from her head. "What do you mean, *we* will light it? *I* will not be here because you said you would take me home. You told Joseph, and he'll tell my family. If I don't arrive soon, they'll start to worry."

He hesitated, and either the candlelight was playing tricks or a flush spread up his neck. "Prior to Joseph's departure, I told him I would bring you home in the sleigh after you warmed up and *if* it stopped snowing. Your family will know not to expect you until after the weather has cleared."

"You did *what*?" Suddenly, her body felt as frigid as the darkening sky beyond the windows. The sky that importuned her by continuing to release a thick curtain of snowflakes, swirled about by the icy wind.

"There have already been enough misfortunes today." His shoulders became a little stiffer, his tone more assured. "I refuse to risk adding to them by allowing you to leave in the midst of a snowstorm. Surely, you see the folly of such an undertaking."

"The only greater folly," she snapped, "would be for me to remain at your house indefinitely!"

"As I said"—his voice became low, although it invited no protest—"I'll bring you home when the snow stops."

She jumped from the yule log as if it had already been set on fire. And it was supposed to bring her luck? *Ha*!

She flounced away, unable to look at the thing any longer. Unable to look at *him*. Instead, she established herself by the window, pressing her heated cheek to the frosty glass.

Blast the snow. Blast the yule log. Blast Nate and his good intentions, and blast the bruises on her heart, and blast, blast, *blast*. Something in her chest vibrated, ready to break out as a scream that would reverberate to the rooftop.

Except what would that accomplish? Would shouting her frustration cause the snowstorm to stop raging? Turn back time so she'd never gone for a walk in the woods? Undo all the years she'd fancied herself in love with Nathaniel Pembrook, only to discover he viewed her as a laughingstock?

She tightened her fingers into fists, well aware of the answer.

And then, because there was nothing else left to do, she pivoted, inclining her head to him in a gesture of perfect gentility. "Thank you, Mr. Pembrook. I'll eagerly await the moment that happens."

One of his golden brows twitched, and while his lips parted, no words came out.

Had she not given him the outraged response he expected? Well, she refused to play into his beliefs by offering any other. She held his gaze, the muscles in her face straining with the effort of maintaining an expressionless veneer.

Let it never be said that her reaction was *childish*.

4

Nate's satisfaction at seeing the yule log in his great hall proved disappointingly short-lived.

At first sight, the object—retrieved and brought in with expediency by one of his two remaining footmen—had seemed to brighten the entire vast, echoing space. Not because there was anything particularly awe-inspiring about a muddy piece of ash wood that remained unlit, but because it represented something more. Namely, progress. A symbol that his endeavor went beyond a total failure.

For a few fleeting moments, sparks of contentment had stirred in his chest. Sparks that had flared into something else —for contentment seemed too weak a word—as Emily lowered herself to the yule log in the pursuit of luck, and all he could think of was that he wished for his oil paints and a healed right hand so he could capture the scene.

Yet the sparks had abruptly disintegrated the instant he let his careless words slip out, thus solidifying the truth of her situation: the snow had left her stranded. Just as he was once more confronted with a dismal truth of his own: the yule log was but a minor accomplishment on a long list of tasks he had neither the resources nor the ability to perform.

He squared his shoulders, returning her ominously cool nod with one of his own. He had no illusions that she'd accepted her fate with gladness. Regretfully, he didn't hold the power to change the weather or turn back time. All he could do was see to her well-being before confronting the myriad tasks that required his attention.

"Allow me to show you to the drawing room," he said. "The fire is lit, and you can repose in comfort after our ... unfortunate experience."

Emily didn't move. "And what will you do while I'm reposing?"

His eyes darted around the great hall, the *greatness* of the room somewhat diminished by the disarray of furniture and miscellaneous items that had been dragged in for the party but not yet set up. Between that, the food, the gifts, the decorating ... how did he decide what to pursue first?

"Assemble the gift baskets, I suppose. One for each servant and tenant family." He made the decision at random, wholly unsure whether it was the right one. At the very least, he should be able to pack baskets without his hand proving him incompetent.

She nodded, a clipped, purposeful gesture. "I'm going to help you."

"You needn't." The words shot out at once, sharper than he'd intended. "You're an unwilling guest in my home, and I refuse to add to your strife by running you ragged besi—"

"I'm going to help you, Mr. Pembrook, because if I don't have something to keep myself occupied, I may well go mad." Her eyes flashed in warning, daring him to contradict her.

Not for the first time that afternoon, he choked back a beleaguered sigh. He hadn't wanted to overwork her, to drag her into more of his predicaments. Hadn't wanted her to keep seeing him struggle. Nevertheless, who was he to turn down help? Especially when so blatantly offered.

"As you wish, my lady." There was no time for an argument, and no other answer for him to give. His hand throbbed as he made the concession, reminding him of the necessity of what he'd agreed to.

He clutched it to his side, taking another minute to survey the clutter alongside the walls. His housekeeper, Mrs. Ruck, had already gathered an array of baskets for his use, although he'd been too shamefaced to ask for advice about what he should place within them. His father had seemed to just *know* these things and execute them perfectly, while Nate plundered along in oblivion. He'd gone to the village earlier in the day to purchase a copious number of sweetmeats, and Mrs. Ruck was upstairs seeking some ribbons and bolts of cloth that had been tucked away in a closet. As for what else to include—

"Preserves," he muttered to himself, a burst of inspiration taking hold. Rosemead's larder was always packed with them at this time of year, and he had a vague recollection of seeing jars in the St. Stephen's Day baskets from years past. "I'm going to the kitchen to get some preserves for the baskets," he clarified, heading back toward the door that led to the servant's stairs.

"I'll fetch them." At once, Emily was in motion, her footsteps falling into a near-run that quickly surpassed his.

No. He stopped the protest from tumbling out just in time. He could tell her she shouldn't, she needn't. Yet which one of them had a useless hand that was apt to send the jars crashing upon the floor?

As the answer to that question was not Lady Emily Prescott, he let her go without another word, watching as she slipped through the door and left him alone to reassess the clutter surrounding him.

The bags of sweetmeats, along with a purse brimming

with coins, rested atop one of the unadorned tables. Surely, he could distribute them amongst the baskets without causing another disaster.

And so, they remained thusly occupied for a long stretch in which the sky turned from dusky gray to pure black, brightened only by the whirling mass of snowflakes. Mrs. Ruck had done an admirable job of locating ribbons, laces, caps, and handkerchiefs, and once Emily had brought in all the preserves —and had been provided with a pair of slippers, also thanks to the housekeeper—she worked in silence to divide everything up.

Behind them, the footmen toiled away, dragging the tables to the center of the room and carrying in chairs from all parts of the house. Nate's eyes, however, seemed incapable of focusing on anything but Emily. She moved gracefully, efficiently, always pivoting in the opposite direction as he made his way along the rows of baskets, completing his trivial task of dropping in sweetmeats and coins.

He didn't interfere with her efforts by attempting conversation she wouldn't want. As the clutter on the floor became neatly arranged piles in baskets, though, he at least needed to make a small overture.

He waited until she deposited a final ribbon before approaching her, holding out the bag that he'd emptied of its contents, aside from two lemon drops.

Perhaps unsurprisingly, she pursed her lips, her dark brows rising in question. Likely in annoyance, too. It *was* just a silly, insignificant gesture on his part. Nonetheless, he didn't back away from it, even as unsettling heat crept up his neck.

"For you." He nudged the bag closer, tilting it so she could see its contents. After so many years of separation, he'd suddenly been hit with the memory that Lady Emily—at least, the younger version of her—had a penchant for sweets. "It's ... it's nothing, really. Merely the paltriest token of my thanks.

Because I am. Thankful, that is. For your assistance where my own efforts proved lacking."

She eyed the bag in that unreadable way of hers. A precursor to the moment she would laugh at the inanity of his gesture and storm away?

She didn't do that, though. Instead, her fingers reached into the bag, and she popped one of the lemon drops into her mouth, motioning for him to take the other.

"There's no shame in needing help," she said at last, her tongue—that enticing flash of pink—running over her bottom lip as she savored the tartness. "And you can hardly fault yourself for being injured."

"Can't I?" A surge of bitterness coated his throat—one that didn't derive from lemon.

She fell silent again, the subtle motion of her jaw as she sucked on the sweetmeat doing odd things to his insides. Until finally, more words, spoken in a tone that was gentler than before. "May I ask what happened?"

He looked away, his gaze traveling downward to the evidence—the bruised, distorted evidence—of his misfortune. "My hand had an encounter with—or should I say, beneath—a large piece of marble."

Her eyes grew wide, the amber depths brewing another multitude of queries. He hadn't given her much of an answer, had he? He'd never *wanted* to speak on the subject with anyone. Yet he and Emily were trapped together with no one else for company. What did he stand to lose by answering the question?

"I'd been painting for the entirety of my grand tour in the Mediterranean," he said, his mind flickering back to turquoise water, whitewashed buildings, *sunshine*. "But when at last I was able to travel to Italy, after the war, I decided to try sculpting as well. As you can see, I didn't succeed."

"Oh ... I'm sorry." She swallowed; the last of her lemon

drop must have melted away. "I can only imagine how upsetting that was. You were fortunate, at least, to have so many years abroad to pursue your artwork at a time when most found themselves unable to leave England's shores."

Fortunate. Reckless, more like. He'd taken the inheritance he'd received from his mother upon his twenty-first birthday and run with it. Not seeking permission. Not caring—not realizing—how his father needed him. He'd spent his years in Greece, and then his brief time in Italy, thinking of nothing but himself. Of his own desires. Of what he wished to escape.

All until fate had demanded he change course.

"Yes." He flicked his uninjured wrist as if it made little difference either way, although he couldn't keep the trace of acrimony from his tone. "Regrettably, my years of pursuing art abroad did nothing to prepare me for assembling St. Stephen's Day gift baskets. My father, who rarely stepped out of England until this summer, is much better at these things than I could ever hope to be."

Her lashes fluttered, her mouth forming a thoughtful little pout. "Why did you return home when he did not? I thought you'd quite abandoned Rosemead and that the two of you were to spend Christmas in France."

"I did, and we were." He shifted so his body leaned against the wall, for an invisible weight had fallen upon his shoulders, the burden of it heavy and exhausting. "But damn me for a fool, all I could think of was the party. The pride my mother took in hosting it. The way my father so seamlessly assumed the management of it after her death. The way the tenants would flock to the great hall to carouse and laugh, and name it as a bright point of their year."

It was funny how those things, which had once only skirted his awareness, had suddenly jumped to the forefront after he'd met with his father in Paris. A reunion that had forced him to confront his ignorance and selfishness. Because his father, for once, had put himself first, leaving Nate with some serious priorities to reassess.

"I could have stayed away as planned." He glanced toward the window, where the world beyond had become nothing but a melee of darkness and snowflakes. "Yet I'd shirked my responsibility as heir to Rosemead for long enough. Somehow, I couldn't allow that to continue. Not for St. Stephen's Day."

Good God, had he really said all that aloud? The following silence alerted him that he'd been speaking for far too long. And too intimately. He'd vowed not to burden her any longer. Didn't want her privy to his innermost failings when he already had plenty in plain sight.

However, the set of Emily's features was soft, and her eyes shone with something much mellower than disdain. "That's ... noble of you."

Her praise created a flicker of warmth within his chest. A single hopeful spark that was promptly doused by the cold weight of the truth. He didn't warrant such a descriptor. He was simply trying to atone.

"I should collect some oranges." He pushed away from the wall. Away from memories and regrets and eyes that heated him like brandy. "For the baskets," he added mindlessly, grabbing a candelabrum and making a rapid retreat toward the corridor without looking back.

Even so, it took only an instant for her footfalls to catch up with his. "Lead the way, and I'll assist you."

He didn't try to refuse her this time, although the temptation did remain. However, she'd insisted, in no uncertain terms, that she needed a distraction, and orange picking was hardly among the most strenuous activities she could undertake.

His main concern was that his poor luck would extend to the orangery, and he'd open the door to find all the greenery brown and wilted. When they entered, though, he was hit by a blast of warm, fragrant air, reminiscent of a summer garden. Rosemead's gardener may have departed the house to spend Christmas elsewhere, but it seemed he'd left things well-tended.

Nate wandered farther inside, shining the light from his candles over the long, narrow space he hadn't entered since ... he didn't remember when. His father had made improvements in the years of Nate's absence, apparently, for more large windows had been added to the south wall, and the roof now contained a glass dome, decorated by creeping vines.

A dome that was ruefully topped by a thick coating of snow. Nonetheless, the plants remained oblivious to the weather beyond the confines of the orangery, for the trees were laden with oranges, and hundreds of fragrant blooms adorned the various flowers and shrubs.

"This is beautiful." Emily tiptoed across the slate tiles, her gaze traveling from floor to ceiling, inspecting all the greenery in between. *Orangery* was perhaps an inapt name for the space, as his parents had taken to cultivating far more than citrus fruit—even pineapples, at one point in time, although Nate didn't spot any presently. Whatever exotic fruits and flowers remained on display, Emily's attention had come to rest upon the roses. "After all the years I visited Rosemead, I cannot believe this was always here, and I never knew it."

She stopped beside a particularly showy rosebush, leaning down to sniff a crimson bloom the size of a dessert plate. Her eyelids drifted closed as she inhaled, her lips forming a delicate upward curve.

Why did he suddenly feel like he, too, was discovering a great many things for the first time?

His jaw twitched, and something stirred deep within his gut. But, unlike her, his eyes remained wide open, not even chancing to blink. The sight of her bent over the rosebush—

not hostile, not guarded, but immersed in a moment of pure pleasure—was too rare, too exquisite, to miss for even a second.

He had baskets to finish packing, decorations to hang, tables to arrange. Yet even the looming time constraints, which had propelled him forward the whole day, couldn't entice him to move.

Not until Emily straightened abruptly, her features becoming shuttered, did his own body follow suit, his eyes darting to the window as if he'd been caught reaching for something he wasn't allowed to have. She abandoned the rose-bushes, starting toward the potted citrus trees along the wall. "Let's gather the oranges."

"Yes. Indeed." His feet waited a beat too long before jerking into motion, his first step unnervingly clumsy as he followed behind her. If he wouldn't risk drawing her attention, he may well be inclined to bang his head against one of the tree trunks and see if he couldn't impart some sense into himself.

Meanwhile, Emily already had two oranges cradled in the folds of her skirt like a makeshift basket, because the woman was nothing if not efficient. If only he could say the same of himself.

He swept his light over the floor until it fell upon an actual basket propped next to one of the wrought iron benches, and he hastily retrieved it, setting it down beside Emily's feet.

Once again, they worked methodically and silently, making their way along the row of orange trees until the basket grew full.

"That should be nearly enough." He peered toward the top of the final tree in the row, where a cluster of oranges remained in the highest branches. "I'll just fetch the ladder so I can get these last few and ensure we don't run short."

"Allow me." She followed his gaze to where a small ladder

rested against the wall between two of the floor-to-ceiling windows, her feet flying across the tiles yet again.

"No." He'd been trying very hard not to gainsay her and instead to show his appreciation for her help. However, he could hardly sit back and watch her climb the creaky old ladder in slippers that may not even fit properly. "There's no need for you to exert yourself. I'll get the oranges."

"Because, even with only *half* your hands in good working order, you think yourself so much more capable of climbing a ladder than I?" Anger turned her eyes into blazing amber orbs. "Stop telling me I *cannot*! I'm not an invalid or a delicate flower. I'm not a *child*."

Her vehemence hit him in the face like a blast of ice. Or perhaps fire. Whatever it was, it filled his veins with a potent mixture of hot and cold, so much so that it was a wonder he didn't stagger again. No, one could hardly accuse her of being delicate when she stood before him with her shoulders squared, her spine rigid, and her chin pointed in defiance.

His mind was a whirl, careening back and forth between the pale-faced girl who used to sit at the dining table on Christmas Eve and the woman who dragged yule logs through the woods and bent down to smell flowers as if she'd never experienced anything so blissful in her life. It seemed there was a fact with which he needed to reconcile himself: the girl was gone. All that remained was the woman.

"No." Lord, his voice sounded gravelly. Muffled. But looking into her eyes—and experiencing the frost, the burn— he could manage nothing better. "Of course you're not."

She tugged the ladder, testing him. When it moved in her direction without resistance, she gave a slight nod, dragging it over to rest against the tree trunk.

He'd conceded, given her what she wanted. However, he'd be damned if he didn't at least hold the ladder in place while she climbed. They exchanged a look while he settled himself against the side of the ladder, taking hold of the rail. Ultimately, she must have deemed this small interference acceptable, for she stepped onto the first rung without another word, her body nimble as she began her ascent.

If her borrowed shoes were too loose or too tight, she gave no indication of it, for she stood on tiptoe partway up the ladder, plucking the final few oranges and dropping them gently into the basket below.

He didn't mean to stare. Only, this angle showed her curves—the contour of her hips, the gentle swell of her backside—to particular advantage. She may be small of stature, but she possessed an almost feline-like grace, her limbs elongating and receding in a seamless cycle.

Limbs that deftly climbed down the ladder until she was on the ground once again, turning to him with a pert dip of her chin. "There. Do you think that will suffice?"

She meant the oranges, of course. Did he think they had enough *oranges*? Except suddenly, he didn't know or care. Her body was close to his, a single footstep away from colliding with his chest. And that didn't suffice at all, because he wanted it closer. Wanted to know how those curves felt without the barrier of her cloak, wanted to transcend the orangery's perfume of flowers to discover her own unique scent. Wanted to know if her lips were soft, if her tongue tasted like lemon drops.

If she realized the direction of his thoughts, this sweet, stubborn, infuriating, *tempting* woman would be apt to slap her palm across his cheek and storm away.

She didn't do that, though. Didn't develop her familiar frown of impatience even when he failed to answer. In fact, her body drew nearer, her chest subtly rising and falling as she peered up at him, her eyes like molten amber, warm honey, the most decadent brandy.

Her lips parted, releasing a scarcely audible trickle of

breath. An exhale that acted as a magnet, causing him to lean forward, for his mouth to lower—

"We should bring these to the great hall and get them distributed." With a single brisk motion, she bent to heft the basket into her arms. "With any luck, the snow will have stopped by the time we're through, and you can ready the sleigh."

She burst out of the orangery and into the chillier air of the corridor, her movements rapid but no longer graceful. However, any protests he'd thought to make about the basket being too heavy were promptly vanquished by her next words.

"I need to get home and greet my betrothed."

5

The words felt wrong the instant they crossed Emily's lips. *My betrothed.* Why had she said that? Why had she gotten ahead of herself in such a manner?

Perhaps because throughout the entire course of her misadventures at Rosemead, not once had her thoughts drifted to Lord Coleville. Not until the moment when her lips had almost collided with Nathaniel Pembrook's, and reality had hit her like a bucket of ice water dumped atop her head.

Foolish. So foolish. Maybe there was something in the air of the lush, beauteous orangery that caused its occupants to lose all sense. Which was precisely why she kept walking, one determined footfall after the other with the heavy basket in tow, until she reached the safety of the great hall. A space that was likewise beautiful but also too stark and chilled to elicit any imprudent actions.

She set the basket of oranges next to the other rows of baskets they'd assembled, taking a moment to discreetly catch her breath. Heaven forbid that Nate notice she'd grown winded.

He hadn't tried to speak while she marched away from the

orangery but had followed with equal briskness, remaining one step behind. Now that they'd stopped, though, she could feel him hovering at her heels. Could sense his gaze on the back of her neck.

"I didn't realize." His voice sounded odd, somehow, almost as if his throat had constricted. "My sincerest congratulations to you both."

She drew in one more quick breath, then pivoted toward him, exertion rendering her cheeks maddeningly hot. Except, if she were being honest with herself, exertion no longer felt like the reason for her flush. "Thank you."

She could have left her speech there. She *should* have turned away from him, seen to the oranges, and counted the minutes until it stopped snowing. Yet the echo of what she'd said seemed to linger in the air, making everything feel disjointed and wrong.

"However ..." The word rested on her tongue a moment, and she had to force her eyes not to turn to the floor. "You can save your felicitations for a later time. I misspoke. Lord Coleville isn't my betrothed *exactly*."

There, she'd replaced the burden of her lie with the truth. Only, why did voicing it make her feel no better? Perhaps because she sounded so ridiculous. And if anything, her skin burned hotter than ever.

Now that she considered it, Nate's face appeared flushed as well. His body too stiff. However, he gave no reaction but a sardonic lift of his brow. "I was unaware that a state existed between having a betrothed and not having one."

Her eyes narrowed, her mouth pinching together at the corners. And she'd almost *kissed* this man? What on earth had she been thinking?

Her spine grew as straight as an iron rod, and she peered at him in a way that would put him in grave danger if looks had the ability to do harm. "Lord Coleville and I have an understanding. He's coming to spend Christmastide at Beaumont Manor. Arriving today, in fact, and the purpose of his visit is no great mystery."

"Ah, I see." Nate's brow lowered again, and while she awaited another quip to follow, it didn't come. Instead, he broke away, meandering toward one of the large windows, where the panes of glass had become covered in hundreds of icy flakes. "Unfortunately, Lady Emily," he said to the stormy blackness beyond, "I don't anticipate the snow stopping anytime soon. As darkness has fallen, and some digging may be required before we can even reach the coach house to fetch the sleigh, I think it would be best if you took a room here for the night and deferred all plans for travel until morning."

Something knocked against the wall of her chest, although it wasn't the blow she would have expected from having her worst fear confirmed. For she'd realized it long before now, hadn't she? As much as she'd kept her eyes on the windows and alluded to her imminent departure throughout their after-noon of basket-filling, she hadn't been so delusional as to think the sky would magically clear, and she would glide home as if in a nighttime winter wonderland.

She'd already stifled her emotions before him once today. The act of doing so again proved decidedly easier this time— so much so that by the time he turned, she'd clasped her hands in front of her and was ready to offer a conciliatory nod. "You're correct. I thank you for extending your hospitality." She impressed even herself with the coolness of her tone.

The cords in his neck moved as he swallowed, the edge of his mouth giving an uncertain tic before he promptly pressed it closed. "Uh, right." He stepped away from the window, the tap of his boots accelerating as he crossed the great hall. "Excuse me a moment while I go speak to Mrs. Ruck to ensure there's a suitable chamber prepared."

"Of course. Thank you." She would throw so much

measured politeness at him that he'd drown in it. Although whether her final rejoinder had caught him off balance, she couldn't say, for he was gone in the blink of an eye, his footsteps fading into the corridor beyond.

She waited—hands still clasped, back still straight—until not even an echo of him remained. And then, with a long, shuddering sigh, she sank to the floor, dropping her forehead into her palms.

The basket of oranges beside her was sweetly fragrant, containing a hint of summer. However, it couldn't take away the endless whirl of snow outside that made leaving Rosemead impossible.

It's all temporary, she assured herself, *and will be rectified come morning*. She closed her eyes, repeating the thought in a steady stream. Tomorrow, her misadventure while holly gathering would exist as nothing but a bad memory, and all would be as it should. She'd be back with her family.

With Lord Coleville.

Because if the snow hadn't impeded him, Lord Coleville would be waiting for her. Lord Coleville, who'd promised in his most recent letter that they would have a Christmastide to remember.

She tried to use that knowledge to drum up warmth—hope—within her chest.

Instead, all she got was hollowness, and a little voice in the back of her head whispering that, maybe, there was a reason she hadn't fought harder to return to Beaumont.

6

When Emily awoke with a racing heart, covered in a sheen of perspiration, the world was cloaked in darkness.

She sat bolt upright in bed, her eyes darting around wildly, struggling to turn all the shadowy shapes into something familiar. Yet there was nothing reassuring. Nothing at all but an ominous rattle as the wind shook the windowpanes.

I'm not in my own bedchamber. The truth came rushing back, pelting her like a blast of icy air. Her vision adjusted to the dimness enough to distinguish bed curtains, a counterpane, pillows. But none of them were hers. This wasn't Beaumont Manor, where her sister, Anna, resided in the bedchamber next door, always willing to keep Emily company when she awoke in one of her *moods*.

She was at Rosemead House. *Alone.*

She pressed a hand to her chest, attempting a few deep breaths. However, the air wouldn't stop rushing in and out of her lungs in short bursts. Likewise, her torso was stiff, and as much as she tried forcing herself to relax, it refused to drop back to the mattress.

She pushed aside the bed curtains, hopping to the floor and feeling about with her feet until she located her borrowed slippers. Sleep would never reclaim her in this state, so why torture herself by attempting it?

Mrs. Ruck had found a dressing gown for her, and she slid it onto her shoulders, hugging the fabric tight to her body as she hurried toward the door. This guest bedchamber, like the rest of Rosemead, was well-furnished and pleasingly decorated, although she suddenly couldn't stay in it a moment longer.

While the fire in her room had died down to weak embers, casting a chill about the space, it was nothing compared to the frostiness that hit her when she entered the corridor. But it didn't matter. She kept going farther into the icy darkness, feeling her way along as she approached the staircase.

Sometimes, when she couldn't sleep at Beaumont, she and Anna would go down to the library, and Anna would read aloud in the most outlandish voice she could manage until Emily's anxieties became laughter. Perhaps she would obtain similar comfort by finding Rosemead's library and sitting for a spell with a book. Or maybe she simply needed to walk until her limbs became cold and tired enough that the demand to rest them overtook her racing thoughts.

She made it down the stairs and through the short corridor that ran to the great hall, which contained doors leading to other parts of the house—the library included, presumably. Not surprisingly, the space held no additional warmth, for the flames in the hearth had diminished to embers here, too.

However, this vast room did have light. *Candlelight*. For sitting at one of the long tables the footmen had dragged to the center of the room was Nate, his hand finagling a branch from the pile of greenery set out before him.

Her muscles seized, her feet halting abruptly. Yes, it was his house, but he wasn't supposed to be here. Not in the middle of the night, still fully alert and wearing the same trousers and waistcoat he had during the day. Once they'd finished meting out the oranges and putting the final touches on the gift baskets, he'd arranged for Mrs. Ruck to show her to her chamber and bring her a tray of simple fare, suggesting that he, too, would retire early so they could awaken and be underway at first light.

Well, his plans had obviously changed—for aside from the fact that he'd removed his coat and loosened his cravat, it didn't look like he'd retired at all. Which left her with a pressing dilemma: what was she to do now? Perhaps she could tiptoe backward with the utmost secrecy, as if she'd never been here—

Except his eyes fell upon her without missing a beat, and suddenly, it was too late.

"Lady Emily." He rose from his seat, tossing the branch— holly, it looked like—back to the table and casting it a wry look. "It's officially Christmas Eve," he offered by way of explanation, his hand sweeping over the array of branches.

Yes, Christmas Eve. The day when decorations could be hung without the threat of bad luck. Why, then, did she keep descending farther into disaster?

"Forgive me." She startled backward a step, away from all the festive greenery. Away from her mistake. From *him*. "I shouldn't have been wandering, I—"

"Rosemead isn't haunted to the best of my knowledge," he cut in, giving his chin an inquisitive tilt to the side, "but you look like you've seen a ghost."

"I haven't, I ..." Blast, why did her voice sound so pitiably shaky? And why did her knees keep trembling beneath her dressing gown?

"What's happened?" He pushed away from the table and made it to her side in a matter of seconds, his brows drawing together in concern. He really was devastatingly handsome—a fact her brain insisted on reiterating, even as apprehension clutched her within its grasp.

She squeezed her eyes shut, willing her heart to stop its rapid thudding. How was she to answer that question without sounding ridiculous? *I had a nightmare. Just like a child.*

"Never mind." His words broke through the pounding in her ears, and his hand fell upon her sleeve, giving it a gentle tug. "Come with me."

His fingertips were sparks, searing her to the bone. A sensation that was ... exhilarating.

A sensation that required prompt dousing. But disquiet, apparently, bred compliance, for before she could think better of it and shake him off, she was striding through the great hall on her shaky legs, allowing him to lead her. He released her for only a moment to retrieve his candelabrum before continuing the trek, taking her through one of the paneled oak doors.

A door that opened to a familiar short corridor, and then, they were back in the orangery, greeted by its aromatic summertime warmth.

She went so far as to let him guide her to a bench beside the rosebushes, where she sank to the wrought iron seat, taking in large mouthfuls of the fragrant air. However, as the heat began to soothe her trembling limbs, her gaze shot upward, tracking him as he turned away to set down the light and pulled at something tucked within his coat. "Why are we here at this time of night?"

"Because you like it here," he answered as if it were the most natural thing in the world, and before she could utter another word, he came back to her, extending a liquor bottle that contained an unknown dark liquid. "Drink this."

She eyed the green-black glass—how had he acquired it without her notice?—and felt her mouth become pinched. Surely, he wasn't serious.

"Go on." He nudged it toward her palm, making the liquid splash within the bottle. "I won't tell a soul."

Drat him, anyway. She accepted the offering, pulling out the stopper and tipping the bottle to her lips before common sense had a chance to reappear. At once, her throat was hit with the potent burn of brandy, a sensation that seeped into her chest and pooled between her ribs. On the limited occasions when she'd sampled her father's brandy, she hadn't thought she liked it. However, she now found something comforting in the fiery liquid, and she took another quick drink before pushing the bottle back at him.

He must be satisfied with her efforts, for he accepted it into his grasp and lowered himself to the opposite side of the bench. "Now," he said, his tone low. Calming. His eyes another source of piercing heat as he assessed her. "Will you tell me what happened?"

She swallowed, her throat still afire. Her head somehow more restful but also more hazed than before. "I couldn't sleep." That was all the answer she needed to give. She could leave it at that, excuse herself, and pace the floor of the guest bedchamber until light streaked through the windows and the snow faded away. However, brandy—or perhaps the very air of this dreamlike orangery—made her tongue limber enough that more words slipped out. "I usually can't in unfamiliar places." *Sometimes, not in familiar places, either.* "Not since ..."

Oh, she'd said too much. Had made herself vulnerable where vulnerability had no place. Yet he continued to look at her, his body shifting forward just the slightest amount. His expression ... thoughtful. *Kind.* "Not since what, love?"

The endearment shot to her heart, equal parts wonderful and devastating. It meant nothing, of course. *Words to placate a frail, quivering child.* Regardless, the truth rose in her throat, no longer content to stay inside and gnaw a hole but insisting it break free.

She drew in a long breath. "Not since the voyage I took as a girl. The one where I became ill, and my mother …"

She trailed off, unable to finish the sentence but also not needing to. All the ton—Nate included, certainly—knew of her mother's affair. Of how Emily had been dragged along as her mother had tried to run away to India with her lover, only for fever to hit each one of them during the voyage and claim her mother's life.

What they didn't know was the story of the twelve-year-old girl who'd lain by herself in bed at night as the ship back to England swayed over the waves, unsure of what ached more: her body or her heart. The girl whose father had tried to offer comfort, but grief and confusion had made her push him away, until all she had left was her broken self and the darkness.

Yet why did she think it wise to trouble Nate—to *trust* him—with all that? She gave her head an abrupt shake, as if she could rid herself of both the memories and her own imprudence. "It's beyond absurd. It all happened so long ago. There's no reason that dreams of those things should still affect me now."

"It's not absurd." He shook his head just as vehemently, and his hand came out, about to fall upon hers, before he seemed to think better of it and placed it in his lap. "Do the dreams plague you often?"

"Not *so* often." She released a soft sigh, allowing her rigid torso to rest against the back of the bench. "They seem to grow worse when I'm already anxious or unsettled." *Such as when I find myself trapped in a house with the man I wished never to see again.*

The thought rose from force of habit. Yet in this moment,

it didn't seem true. Being sequestered in the orangery with Nate felt ... *safe*.

"Try not to worry." He straightened a little, flashing a half-smile that didn't quite meet his eyes. "The snowstorm is bound to exhaust itself soon, and I'll have you back at Beaumont—and with your *almost* betrothed—by morning."

"It's not ..." *It's not that.* She'd already snapped those words at her sister today when Anna teased her about Lord Coleville. Why did Nate, too, have to make that assumption?

More pertinently, perhaps: why couldn't the assumption be true? Why couldn't all her troubles be solved by a reunion in Lord Coleville's arms? By a Christmastime proposal? By a future where everything was sensible and planned?

A shadow passed over Nate's face, along with a small tic in his jaw. He lifted the brandy bottle to his lips, taking a long swig before setting it back on the ground. "Is it a love match?"

And just like that, the warmth in her belly dissipated; her crumbling defenses shot right back up. "You're very forward, Mr. Pembrook. I'm not sure why that's pertinent to you."

"Ah." Traces of brandy shone upon his lips. A knowing glint flickered in his pupils. "So, *no*."

"How dare ..." Her voice came out too loud, too defensive, and she pressed her mouth closed before her speech could escalate into a full-blown diatribe. Instead, she seethed in silence, her fingernails digging into the folds of her borrowed dressing gown. He had no right to make that sort of presumption. No right to voice it so casually.

Except ... he wasn't wrong. He discerned too much, could see all the way through to her heart. How could she condemn him for speaking the truth?

Even if the truth hurt.

She leaned over, taking another swallow of brandy before sitting back up to hold his gaze. "It's not as simple as that," she said, gratified by the composure in her tone. "After one has had five Seasons, and turned down twice as many proposals for the very reason that they do *not* involve love, one begins to consider the matter differently."

One of Nate's golden brows arched in that familiar, aggravating way. "And how does one consider it, exactly?"

She folded her arms across her chest, contemplating. She could still recall the hopeful determination she'd felt upon making her debut. If her powers of observation had taught her anything, it was that the lack of affection between her mother and father had rendered them miserable, whereas the true love shared between her father and Phoebe made them happy and whole. Therefore, Emily would accept nothing but the latter.

At least, that's what she'd told herself at age eighteen. A conviction she'd tried to uphold throughout the numerous dances, the carriage rides in the park, the whispered words at the theater, when her heart could summon nothing beyond the mildest tug for any of the men who tried courting her. Until eventually, she'd had to ask herself if her beliefs about love were misguided. If, although her body had healed from the long-ago illness, something inside her remained broken.

She quietly cleared her throat, keeping her hands clamped tight around her elbows. "One knows not to expect that every encounter with a gentleman will leave one's head feeling as if filled with champagne and one's stomach filled with butterflies. One instead thinks of a gentleman's character. Of if he's sensible, respectable, and chivalrous."

That sounded trite, even to her own ears. Nonetheless, she wouldn't let him see her cower from her opinions now. "I'm pleased to say that Lord Coleville possesses all these qualities. He inherited his title recently, and unexpectedly, yet he has taken on the role with impeccable finesse. Both my father and uncle esteem him highly and hope to have him as an ally in Parliament." Because if she couldn't have champagne and butterflies, why not form a union that would benefit her family? Where perhaps affection would grow over time.

Nate made a sound that wasn't altogether polite. "I'm not sure that's a good reason to accept a proposal."

"It's as good a reason as any." The line of her mouth grew severe, and her eyes became slits. "Certainly better than basing one's choices on a delusion. After all, what do I know about love? I once fancied myself in love with *you*." She laughed, the sound creating a bitter echo.

"You what?" His shoulders turned simultaneously stiffer and squarer, while his jaw seemed to grow loose at the hinges.

She wished she could take it back. Wished that this blasted orangery didn't make her so free with her words. But at the same time ... there was an odd sort of relief from having that burden unloaded. Therefore, she didn't shy away. "After all the Christmas Eves where we sat across the table from each other, don't tell me you didn't know. I'm certain that my ridiculous blushes, smiles, and giggles made it obvious."

And still, the infuriating man said nothing, merely stared at her with a crease between his eyes, as if he'd never truly *seen* her before.

"You *did* know," she insisted, the ring of his dismissive chortle reverberating through her memory. "But I was only a simpering, sickly *child*."

Something flashed over his features. A dark glint in his eye, a twitch of his mouth. *Comprehension.* "I suppose I did." His exhale came out in an unsteady stream, and if she wasn't imagining things, a hint of a flush spread above his drooping cravat. "Emily ... I wasn't a happy person back then. Nor was I a considerate one. I wasn't in a place to appreciate those sentiments, and I certainly didn't deserve them."

She shrugged, as if it made little difference. As if she'd never been a sixteen-year-old girl who'd fled to her bedchamber on Christmas Eve and cried herself to sleep. "It wasn't real love, of course. How would a girl that age know the true meaning of such a thing? I'm not certain I comprehend it even now. Perhaps, except in the rarest cases, it's naught but an illusion."

Somewhere along the way, his body had shifted closer to hers. Close enough that instead of just the fragrance of flowers, she could detect shaving soap, or cologne, or whatever it was that made him smell deliciously male. She could hear the rush of his breath when his lips parted and knew, by the shape they formed, what he was about to say. *No.*

"I should go back to bed before I turn altogether maudlin," she said in a rush, promptly drowning his refusal. She didn't want him to tell her she was wrong. Didn't want his placating, or anything else from him at all. She inclined her head, adopting her practiced expression of polite neutrality. "But I do feel better than when I awoke, so I thank you, Mr. Pembrook, and apologize again for disturbing you at this hour."

"Wait." Nate's words—and the outward dart of his hand —stopped her just as she began to push to her feet.

And because they were still in the orangery, where the air smelled sweet and the tiles were warm beneath her slippers despite the icy snowflakes that pelted the glass, she obeyed.

He was the one to rise instead, poking about the orangery with the candelabrum in hand. But just as she was about to question what he was doing, he returned with a pair of shears, turning to the rosebush beside her. The one with the beautiful, vibrant blooms she'd earlier recognized as Slater's Crimson and hadn't been able to resist stooping to inhale.

The candelabrum returned to the ground. The blades of the sheers clinked together. And then, he was back sitting on the bench, tucking a lavish scarlet rose behind her ear.

"What's this?" Her posture became rigid; her insides, melting wax. Because his fingertip was brushing along her ear, a featherlight touch that lingered a second or two—or an eternity—before his hand came away, suspended in midair.

"I thought you might enjoy it." He paused, something in his throat seeming to catch. "I thought ... it would suit you."

He was looking at her—they were looking at each other—so deeply. So closely. Like he wished to discern her thoughts. Like he could sense her heart ready to beat out of her chest.

Which was why she stood abruptly, her feet already moving backward—away from rosebushes and lulling heat that provided a false sense of security. "Thank you again, Mr. Pembrook. I'll bid you goodnight."

She didn't wait for his farewell before she pivoted and fled. Just as well, for as it turned out, she didn't think he uttered one. Only silence followed her as she bolted out of the summerlike haven.

Silence, until the wind rattled the glass, and with it came a murmur she couldn't be certain was real. A murmur that was stifled as she threw open the door to the corridor, and winter's chill inundated her once more.

A murmur that stayed with her, nevertheless, as she fumbled through the dark, surrounded by the fragrance of the Slater's Crimson. As she remembered the fragrance of *him*.

I was a damn fool.

7

N ate's first thought, upon cracking an eye open, was that his back hurt.

His back hurt, and an agreeable leafy smell wafted around him.

That, and a sea of green was coming into focus, for the room was bathed in dreary gray light.

Daylight.

He scrambled up to a sitting position, blinking rapidly as he absorbed his surroundings. It was *supposed* to be the middle of the night, when sleeplessness had led him to the great hall so he could start work on decorating. Yes, there'd been a moment—several hours after the orangery incident, which was quickly returning to him with startling clarity— when he went to the row of padded chairs the footmen had lined up along one wall, thinking he would just sit there for a spell.

He certainly hadn't intended to stretch out on the chairs and fall asleep. Especially until ... until ... He fumbled in his pocket for his watch, pulling the face before his bleary eyes.

Until *noon*? He jumped upright, giving his waistcoat a few

tugs and shoving the disheveled clumps of too-long hair off his forehead.

Which was the precise moment he noticed the indecipherable amber gaze upon him. Emily sat at the same table where he'd stationed himself during the night, except instead of his jumble of poorly twisted branches, she held a fully formed kissing bough made of holly and ivy, adorned by red berries and a single apple.

"I took the liberty of finishing this for you," she said without preamble, laying it out on the table for his inspection. "Perhaps you'd like to select a location to hang it."

Yes, and perhaps she'd assist him in doing so. Perhaps they'd stand together beneath the kissing bough, and her lips would draw close to his, just as they had in the orangery.

The orangery, where he'd peered at her in the darkness, and a sensation he couldn't name had set a vise upon his heart. Where he'd thought again of painting and known that even if he no longer had the ability to put it on canvas, he desired the image of that crimson rose against her raven hair to be burned into his memory.

Which it was, most assuredly, although the moment had vanished far too soon, and he'd been left alone amongst the potted shrubs to consider yet another way in which his former self had erred.

He blinked again, fighting through the haze left behind by unrestful sleep, half-wondering why she hadn't jostled him awake come first light. Yet a single glance toward the windows provided the answer. The snow continued to fall with as much intensity, if not more, as the day before, tossed about by the raging wind.

A fact she seemed to accept with remarkable equanimity. That, or she had a particular talent for concealing her true emotions—which was the likelier scenario, now that he thought about it.

"Thank you," he managed, trying to push all thoughts of candlelit orangeries from his head so he could focus. "I will. Later. For now, I should"—he hurriedly contemplated the numerous tasks requiring his attention—"go to the kitchen to ensure Mrs. White has everything she needs."

"I'll join you and see if there's anything I can carry up." She pushed back her chair, casting him a glance that dared him to contradict her as she rushed toward the servant's stairs.

Truth be told, he hadn't regained his senses enough to react quite that swiftly. Nor was he in a position to turn her down. Not after he'd been idiotic enough to sleep the morning away.

He lurched into motion as if he'd received an invisible kick to the arse, a flood of greenery rushing past him as he strode to catch up with her. Not the disordered mass of greenery he'd left behind last night, either, but neatly laid boughs adorning the tables and mantelpiece. She'd been busy, apparently. As had the footmen, for chairs for the guests now lined every wall, and certain tables had place settings.

The satisfaction that arose from the sight of progress proved almost enough to supersede his hot-faced shame at having stayed asleep while everyone worked around him.

Unfortunately, the scene that greeted them in the kitchen did nothing to improve his satisfaction and everything to make his stomach sink toward his boots. The cook, Mrs. White, was adamantly whispering something to the kitchen maid, Sally, who listlessly sliced parsnips at the worktable, her face blotchy and nose bright red.

"Mrs. White? Sally?" He stepped forward, the sound of his boots against the floor making them jump to alertness.

"Oh!" Mrs. White bobbed a quick curtsey, although she couldn't mask the flush that spread over her cheeks, and her brow remained heavily creased. "I mean, good day, sir. Lady Emily. How may we assist you?"

He didn't answer. Didn't have the opportunity, for Emily crept forward, cocking her chin as she eyed the kitchen maid. "Are you unwell, Sally?"

"No, m'lady." The maid shook her head, the croakiness of her words betraying them as a lie. For that matter, her whole countenance betrayed her, from her stooped shoulders to her unsteady feet.

Emily frowned, turning first to Mrs. White and then to him. "She needs to rest, not be in the kitchen."

Sally sniffled pitiably. "I can't. I have too much work to—"

"Quite right," Nate cut in, even as his head spun with the implications of this fresh setback. Yet he could hardly work the poor ill girl to the point of collapse. "My order is that you spend the rest of the day in bed and remain there for however long it takes until your health is restored. Mrs. White, perhaps you could get her a tisane."

"If ... if that's what you wish, sir." Mrs. White curtseyed again, her furtive glance about the kitchen saying everything her words did not: *and how do you think the food for the party will ever be prepared now?*

Her opinions aside, she shuffled Sally out of the kitchen without another word, leaving him behind to watch their departure and then bite back a curse.

He marched across the room, unbolting the exterior door and giving it a halfhearted push. Except his efforts yielded no results beyond a slight creak of the hinges. He tried again, and when met with the same outcome, he put his whole body into the endeavor, slamming his shoulder against the wood.

The effect being that the door shuddered open about half a foot, into a snowdrift, while a blast of icy wind pelted him in the face.

Damn. He stood in the doorway frozen—both figuratively and literally—as he surveyed the utter desolation, the *whiteness*, of the landscape beyond. Then again, what did he expect? That a gaggle of kitchen maids would be outside in the snow, waiting for him to usher them in and grant them the privilege of working in his kitchen on Christmas Eve?

At this rate, he'd be shoveling for hours before he could even reach the stables, let alone ride off to the village to search for a last-minute replacement. In a snowstorm. At yuletide. And that didn't begin to address the problem that the roast geese promised him by Mrs. Hodges at Beaumont would certainly no longer be coming today. The problem that, likewise, he had no means of fulfilling his promise to bring Emily home.

He slammed the door shut again, his face frigid and his nerves significantly more frayed than when he'd opened it ten seconds prior.

But if Emily had noticed the bleakness of the scene outside, she didn't show it, for she moved to the worktable with perfect composure. "I'll assume Sally's place slicing the parsnips." She took up the paring knife, shooting him a measured look. "I'm aware that I *needn't*. That I *shouldn't*. However, there's no one else here to accomplish the task, and I presume I'm not so incapable that I would fail at cutting a few root vegetables."

"You ..." His mouth opened and then closed again. When his mind had flashed to the urgency for a new kitchen maid, he'd never considered a marquess's daughter as a candidate. Yet everything she'd said was true. In fact, she'd begun the task already, her slices not nearly as quick and even as Sally's but still remarkably impressive.

Which left him with just one answer to give. "Thank you." His debt to her—not to mention his awe of her—seemed to be growing by the hour. He'd do better to admit it than fight it. "I only hope my own abilities prove half as proficient."

He came up beside her at the worktable, taking over the space where Mrs. White had left behind a pile of partially chopped onions. He'd peeled and cut apples before. How different could this be?

She glanced up from her task, watching with those warm brandy eyes as he retrieved Mrs. White's knife and pressed it into the pungent white vegetable. It felt odd within his left hand, cumbersome and not altogether steady. Nevertheless, he kept going, establishing an awkward sort of rhythm until the onion—one of them anyway—lay on the worktable in small pieces.

On to the next one, then. He cut off the bottom and began removing the peel, as meanwhile, Emily remained hard at work beside him, her attention wholly engrossed in the parsnips. There was something calming about the steady tap of her cuts. Something that, after the brief setback, once again felt like progress.

He set his knife back into the onion while trying to follow her tempo, his mind trifling with the idea that perhaps his lack of kitchen maids was a surmountable obstacle after all. *Thanks to Emily.*

His eyes darted sideways, unable to keep from looking at her. Concentration made her worry her lip between her teeth, creating an alluring flash of plush pink against white. As for her hair, she'd knotted it into a loose braid that fell down her back and secured it with a ribbon not so different in color from the rose she'd allowed him to slide behind her ear.

She may be small and fine-boned, but she was also powerful. Proficient. So achingly beautiful.

How had he failed to appreciate her in his youth? To at least *consider* what a future with her could look like, when they each grew older, instead of dismissing the idea outright. How had he erred so badly that he now had the ring of her bitter laugh in his ears and words that pressed an uncomfortable weight upon his chest? *I once fancied myself in love with you—*

A stab of pain rushed through his finger, causing his knife to clatter to the worktable.

She stopped her rhythmic chopping motions at once and peered up at him, her lips pursing. "Mr. Pembrook?"

Damn it, he'd cut himself. A slash of red rose on his smallest finger, the accompanying throb serving to emphasize his folly. "It's nothing," he bit out between gritted teeth, a long string of obscenities—all directed at himself—overtaking his thoughts.

"Your hand! You're bleeding," she exclaimed, her eyes following his down to the cut as the trickle of red reached the surface and spilled over.

He at least thought to jerk his hand away from the worktable before his blood dripped onto the onions. Unfortunately, it was too late to undo the rest of his incompetency.

"It's nothing," he repeated gruffly, clutching his damaged finger, a stream of sticky warmth spreading over the palm of his previously injured hand.

Whether or not it was *nothing*, Emily darted away and was back just as quickly with a kitchen towel, shoving it toward him before he could begin bleeding upon the floor.

"I'll be right there with some linen," Mrs. White called from across the kitchen, because naturally, she'd chosen that precise moment to return.

He pressed the towel against his fingers, uncertain if he'd find greater benefit from drumming his head against the bricks of the hearth or going outdoors and burying it beneath a snowdrift. However, he didn't have the opportunity to find out either way, for Emily's arm fell upon his, guiding him forward until they were suddenly at the same chair before the fire where he'd set her down yesterday. She gave him an unsubtle push, the abruptness of it enticing him to sit before he could even think to protest that doing so was unnecessary.

Mrs. White appeared, laden with a basin of water, scissors, ointment, and enough linen to cover his full arm three times over. After a few murmured words from Emily, she set down her bundle and hurried away, leaving Emily to kneel before him. To cradle his hand tightly within hers.

A sensation he couldn't even enjoy, for the heat of the fire in the hearth mixed with the burn of his frustration—his shame—to create an inferno that was altogether stifling.

He cleared the dryness from his throat, producing a sound that had regrettable similarities to a growl. "There's no need for this fuss. I'm—"

"It will only take a moment." She peeked beneath the towel and, seemingly satisfied, started the meticulous task of peeling it away.

He sat rigidly, watching her work with an odd sort of fascination—because he didn't want attention if this was the cause, but he also couldn't move or look elsewhere. His finger, while covered in blood, no longer appeared to be actively bleeding, which he supposed he should count as a victory. Yet it was hard to think of it as such when the gash to his pride remained open and festering.

"You look as somber as if you've just done battle with Napoleon." She dipped the clean edge of the towel into the basin, pausing just long enough to meet his eyes before patting it against his bloodied skin. "Not to worry. I'm certain this will heal quickly."

"My finger isn't the problem," he muttered. Her strokes were so gentle, so delicate. A striking contrast to the tension in his chest and throbbing in his head, which refused to let him give in to the pleasure of her touch. "I shouldn't have been so inattentive. Shouldn't have stayed awake half the night trying to fashion a kissing bough. Shouldn't have slept the morning away and gotten off course."

Which was it: did he feel angry at himself for sleeping not

long enough or *too* long? He didn't know. Perhaps it was a combination of both, along with the countless other regrets that wouldn't stop grating at him. *Shouldn't have broken my hand, shouldn't have run off to the Mediterranean, shouldn't have been so damn ignorant of everything but my selfish whims.*

"You needn't be so severe with yourself. An accidental slip of the hand could have happened regardless of when, where, or how much you slept." She abandoned the towel in favor of the linen, making a precise cut and dabbing on a little of the ointment. "The party preparations will still get done one way or another."

No thanks to him. No thanks to the weather, either, which would impede the tenants from coming if the storm didn't soon relent. Which, somehow, was also beginning to feel like his fault.

He clenched his jaw, following the adept movements of her fingers as she wound the linen over his cut, then tied it securely in place. Once again, she'd come to his rescue. Undone another of his mishaps.

Her brandy-colored eyes darted back up to his face, and for a moment, she was neither working nor releasing his hand but simply looking at him with her palm beneath his fingertips.

I once fancied myself in love with you. The echo of her words wouldn't stop careening through his head. Specifically, the derisive lilt to them, as if she couldn't believe she'd ever harbored sentiments so absurd.

Why hadn't he been a different person back then?

Why wasn't he a different person now: competent instead of lacking?

He stood briskly, pressing his newly bandaged hand to his side and squaring his shoulders. "Thank you. I should return to the great hall and see to the last of the decorating." Surely, he could hang a small bit of greenery without causing another disaster.

He didn't miss the way her hand stiffened, even though the movement was slight. "Very well. I'll get back to the parsnips." She pushed to her feet, swooping down to retrieve the leftover supplies and marching toward the worktable without another word.

Leaving him to watch the swish of her skirts before giving himself another figurative kick into action and rushing toward the great hall to decorate. To get back to progressing and put the mishap behind him.

The finger mishap, at any rate.

He climbed the stairs by taking one rigid, methodical step after another, his finger dully throbbing from the cut. His entire hand prickling from the lingering heat of her touch.

An ache for something that could have been but wasn't.

If he put it in perspective, his accident with the knife was only a small one, apt to make little difference in the end. But as for all the other ways he'd blundered ...

Perhaps there was no coming back from those.

8

"Is something the matter, sir?" Daniel, one of Nate's two loyal footmen, ceased adjusting the fir branch he'd placed in one of the great hall's alcoves and was looking at him strangely.

"Not a thing." Nate gritted his teeth, giving the kissing bough a final tug to straighten it and jumping down from the chair he'd been using to reach the top of the high doorframe. Meanwhile, he fought the overwhelming urge to claw at the skin on his hands until it turned raw.

With his feet planted back on the floor, he took a moment to breathe, clenching his fingers into fists. It was the most damnable thing. The cut on his finger no longer smarted. His broken hand was no stiffer or more painful than usual.

Instead, something worse was happening: both hands felt as if he'd thrusted them into a nest of fire ants—*after* spending the night with them wrapped amongst linens infested with bedbugs.

Which was impossible. Rosemead had neither ants nor bedbugs, and he hadn't even slept in a bed last night. Regardless, the itching had started around the time he'd climbed onto the chair to hang the kissing bough and had grown fierier with each passing second. He'd *tried* not to react as if he were a mongrel covered in fleas. However, Daniel's reaction led him to think he hadn't been entirely successful in that regard.

"Mr. Pembrook?" A voice floated up from behind him. *Her* voice, accompanied by the tap of her slippers as she crossed the great hall.

He turned stiffly, his fingers still clamped at his sides— because he would *not*, under any circumstances, scratch his palms in Emily's presence.

The sight of her—the unraveling braid, the plump lips, the pale green muslin that clung to her in all the right places— offered him a moment of reprieve. Now, if he could just focus on that and *not* the hellfire shooting over his skin.

"Mrs. White and I made considerable progress in the kitchen," she said, brushing a loose ebony lock away from her face as she walked. "Franny, your chambermaid, was good enough to join, and ..."

She trailed off, her gaze traveling up and down his body, her lips twisting into a frown akin to Daniel's. He didn't mean for his hand to jerk, but the damnable itch made it impossible for him to keep still. The movement was quick, a momentary loosening of his fingers. Nonetheless, it was enough to make her eyes widen and her mouth fly open. "Your hand!"

Sadly, it wasn't the first—or even the second—time she'd had cause to utter such an exclamation. But while the misfortunes with his hands were becoming an almost laughably common occurrence, that didn't stop her from running over to him. Didn't stop her brow from creasing in concern as she took in the red splotches that had spread as far as his knuckles. "What's happened?"

"Nothing's happened." He folded his hands back into fists —thinking of icehouses, snowstorms, *anything* but the prickling burn that demanded scratching—before approaching the dwindling pile of stray greenery upon the floor. "I hung the kissing bough you made, and now, I'm going to hang these last few branches of ivy, after which I believe we can consider the great hall sufficiently decorated."

He retrieved the ivy, vaguely aware that instead of responding to him, she was murmuring something to Daniel. But the task of holding the branch within his ravaged palms—and not flinching—proved so consuming that the exact nature of her words escaped him.

He surveyed the room until his eyes fell upon an alcove devoid of decorations, and he set it as his target, marching forward with unnaturally rigid steps.

Until suddenly, Emily's voice called out to him again, this time an urgent cry. "Put that down!"

A splendid idea. One that could be made better only if she suggested he proceed by running outdoors and plunging his hands into the nearest snowbank. Yet his wants were beside the point.

He tightened his grip on the ivy branches, even though every nerve ending screamed in protest. "I don't have time to—"

"You're likely having an adverse reaction to the greenery." Once again, she rushed to his side, her chin set in a stubborn little tilt. "You seemed to do well enough with the holly and fir, so unless you've been handling something else entirely, it must be the ivy."

"That's imposs ..." The rebuttal died on his tongue. He'd collected branch after branch in the woods, had stayed up half the night trying to finagle them into the pleasing arrangements his parents had always created. *But not ivy.* He shot a glance at the innocuous-looking leaves within his grasp. The footmen must have gathered these at some point along the way. In fact, Daniel had been hanging them throughout the afternoon without incident. Just as Emily had twisted ivy into the kissing bough—devoid of her gloves, he might add—and appeared no worse for wear.

But for Nate, it was a different story. Of course it was. Poor luck seemed intent on following him like a storm cloud above his head.

Well, he couldn't let that deter him. He was *so* close to completing another task, and he'd be damned if he—

"For heaven's sake!" Emily's hands shot out, wrenching the ivy from his grip and tossing it to the floor. "Do you *want* to do yourself further harm?"

It was a simple question with an obvious answer, but his brain had grown incapable of forming a response. As it turned out, he was spared the trouble, for Daniel scurried back into the room with his arms full, splashing water onto the floor from the basin he carried.

Another basin. Another towel. Another bottle of ointment. Because, once again, the incompetent poor-substitute for a master of the house had blundered.

Nate crossed his arms, his eyes following Daniel as the footman pushed aside a holly branch to make room for the supplies atop one of the long tables. It was but a small reversal of progress, something he could easily fix. Nonetheless, Nate's jaw tightened.

"This will help." Emily rushed over to the table, pulling out the chair closest to the basin and motioning for him to sit.

His hands itched, stung, and burned, desperate for any sort of balm they could come by. Even so, he didn't rush to join her but forced his feet to maintain the same stiff, measured steps as before. Daniel, seeming to sense that Nate didn't require or want an audience, was quick to take his leave into the servant's corridor and shut the door behind him. And still, Nate kept his fingers clamped together and his footfalls slow, until he reached the side of the table and could peer into the flecked, murky mixture in the basin.

His brow rose. "Oatmeal?"

"Yes," she said a little breathlessly, giving her foot an impatient tap against the floor. "Anna had a similar experience to yours one time while cutting hydrangeas, and she claimed that soaking in oatmeal helped immensely."

He didn't doubt her. But he also didn't sit. He didn't know if he could without jumping out of his skin. Since his return to England two days prior, his pride had been bruised, kicked, and trampled. Why was it, then, that his burning hand and this bowl of soggy oatmeal hurtled him over the edge, pushing him beyond the point of what he could abide?

"Thank you," he choked out, summoning the final shred of good manners he had left, "but I don't need it. As I said, I have to finish—"

"Why can you not readily accept my help?" She gave the back of the chair an exasperated shove before planting her hands upon her hips. Gone was the careful mask, the temperate voice that concealed her true emotions. Instead, the woman he'd encountered in the woods had returned with all her blazing indignation. She marched up to him, jabbing a finger in the center of his chest. "Is it because I'm a woman? Because you think I'm a sickly, silly *child*?"

"Because it reminds me of what a bloody failure I am!" He didn't mean to raise his voice, but the words shot out unbidden, replete with every shred of his frustration, his regret, his shame.

Something inside him seemed to break like a wave crashing against the shore, leaving him both inundated and drained. He gave in, sinking to the chair, letting his fingernails trail along his palms as he slowly unclenched his fists.

"Mr. Pembrook. *Nate*." She spoke his name gently, placatingly, as if *he* were the child—and based on his outburst, he very well deserved the title. "I know how much the St. Stephen's Day party means to you, and I can appreciate your frustration with the continued setbacks. However, you cannot keep torturing yourself over every detail and pushing yourself until you're worn to the bone. If things don't work out exactly as they should, the world won't end. There will be other Christmastides, other parties. For it is, after all, just a party."

"But it's not." He blew out a long exhale. And then, because he didn't have the will to fight anymore, didn't know how to claw himself back up from the weariness, he let his hands drop into the basin of watery oats. Lowered his voice so that it wasn't accusatory but simply gave a bland statement of the truth. "You *don't* know what it means to me."

He waited for her lips to thin, for her eyes to flash with anger. But instead, she dropped onto the chair next to him, her face back to that impassive mask, save for the lingering flush in her cheeks. "Tell me, then."

Tell me. As if it were that easy to expose every one of his mistakes, every one of his regrets.

Yet what had the past few days been if not an exercise in keeping him humble? In making him confront his shame and inadequacy head-on. Didn't she deserve to know why he'd been toiling like a madman, and in turn, she toiled along with him?

He'd known her for all her life as his neighbor. The daughter of his father's longtime friend. Now, he also knew her as the woman who'd sat in his orangery in the middle of the night and allowed herself to be vulnerable. What if he could trust her, as she'd trusted him?

He stretched his fingers to the bottom of the basin, the combination of tepid water and oats creating a sensation upon his inflamed skin that nearly approached relief. He basked in it for a moment, his eyelids drifting shut as he gathered his thoughts. And when he opened them again, he was ready.

"Many would consider being the only son of a viscount an enviable position," he began, peering into the cloudy water as if it contained images of the past. "I grew up wanting for nothing. I went to Eton and then Cambridge knowing that when I finished my studies, I would be required to *do* nothing but learn a thing or two about estate management, receive an allowance, and wait for the day when Rosemead would become mine."

He looked up, finding her liquid amber gaze fixed intently upon him. Silently encouraging him to continue. "What more could I have asked for?" he said. "My father always kept Rosemead well-managed and prosperous. He himself is the picture of respectability, esteemed by all who know him. As was my mother, while she lived. I once heard them referred to as the most affable couple in all of England."

He paused, an ache shooting between his ribs as he considered what the pretense must have cost them. "And yet, it wasn't real. They were so polite in the way they interacted with one another, so flawless in how they presented themselves to society. But neither of them was happy, not truly. I could see that even as a child."

He swallowed, trying to push away the memory of the muffled sobs he'd chanced to hear, at different points in time, behind the closed door of both the viscountess's and viscount's chamber. "There was something missing, something not right. Something I couldn't understand, only ... I *knew* I didn't want that to become my life. Visions flashed in my head of the impeccable household I would run, of the reputable wife I'd have beside me, of the admiration we'd receive for how damn perfect we were. Except it would all be a facade to conceal the emptiness beneath. I refused to stay in England and allow that to happen."

He unthinkingly made a gesture with his hand, causing water to splatter over the edge of the basin. Which consequently reminded him that he was perched at a dining table, baring his soul while soaking in oatmeal.

He snapped his hands out of the soupy mixture, sitting a little straighter in his chair. He was saying too much, becoming too open, and looking ridiculous while doing it. Yet here was Emily, not scornful or mocking but leaning forward to pass him a towel, her expression still placid.

He accepted the offering and wiped off his fingers one by one, gratified to find that the urge to scratch his skin raw had abated. As again, an idea prodded at the edge of his thoughts: *you can trust her*.

He set his hands on the table. Peered into the warmth of her eyes. Until suddenly, his words poured out once more. "When my mother died of fever, not long before your own, she left me an inheritance, to be given when I turned one-and-twenty. A tidy sum, and my father offered plenty of suggestions for practical investments I could make once the funds came into my possession. I didn't heed his advice, though. Instead, I took the money and boarded a ship to the Mediterranean."

"Your grand tour," she murmured, reaching for the bottle of ointment.

"Yes. If Lord Byron could do it, why couldn't I?" He had to laugh at himself and his youthful logic. At the young man —the boy, really—who thought little of the dangers of traveling during wartime and even less of his responsibilities at home. "Off I sailed to Greece without companions or tutor. Without a word to anyone, my father especially, for he never would have condoned it. He told me as much when his letters began reaching me, and he begged me to rethink what I was doing and come home. But I didn't, of course."

His chest tightened with a throb of guilt, and his fingers pressed against the tabletop, his nails digging into the oak.

Except then, her hand was upon his, coaxing it to relax, transferring something cool and soothing. The ointment.

His breath stuttered, the gentle circular motions of her fingertips radiating through him, providing a reprieve from the knots that twisted in his gut. Enough that he could keep speaking, as much as he didn't want to.

"I didn't listen," he said dully, feeling the familiar burn of shame creep up his neck, "and while I know I disappointed him, my father didn't try forcing me to do otherwise. Once I made it clear I had no intentions to return anytime soon, he stopped with the imploring and wrote periodic letters only to ensure I was well. And damn me for a fool, I ignored everything I left behind. I suppose I just assumed that the impeccable Lord Pembrook would keep managing the estate as he always did. Whatever misery he concealed, he fit so seamlessly into the role of viscount that he seemed almost eternal. In any case, I didn't make the future my concern. I cared only that I'd escaped Rosemead's curse of false happiness and that I was free to explore the world."

He paused to study Emily's face, waiting for her brow to grow severe or her lips to purse in condemnation. However, she remained focused on the task of rubbing ointment into each patch of his reddened skin, her fingers working in calming circles. Not that he doubted for a minute she was listening.

Very well, then. He may as well finish the story. Reveal the worst of his selfishness.

"Perhaps I could consider my actions more forgivable had I stayed away for a year or two, gotten my fill of painting, and then returned to Rosemead to take on my responsibilities as heir. But after vowing for all my youth that I wouldn't succumb to that fate, I let obstinacy keep me away long after the thrill of the voyage wore off." He sighed, a low sound of regret for the things to which he'd been oblivious back then.

Which were so obvious now. "Even the news I received from my father at the beginning of summer—that he was departing Rosemead for an extended stay in France—didn't make me rethink my decision. It took a slab of marble crushing my hand to do that."

A single moment of carelessness that had caused everything in his life to change. "With my lackluster attempts at sculpting no longer an option, I joined my father in Paris. Miraculously, he welcomed me instead of disowning me. And finally, after so many years apart, we had a conversation. One that helped me understand ..."

His throat constricted, making the last of his words sound pinched. "He told me that he and my mother had cared for and valued each other as friends, but that theirs was a marriage of convenience. She'd been betrothed to another who was killed in a carriage accident, and when rumors began circulating about her virtue, she needed to marry elsewhere or risk facing ruin. My father was there to step in, and it seems they came to a mutually beneficial arrangement. Nonetheless, her heart forever belonged to the man she lost. And as for my father ..."

He stopped again, an ache building in his gut. After all the years where his father had shown him only a pleasant mask, it had been difficult to sit in those rented rooms in Paris and listen while the cordial viscount talked of secrets and sorrow. It was difficult to think of it even now. Nate had been so consumed by his own wants and fears that he'd never taken time to consider *why* his parents were unhappy. He'd never truly *known* his father. He should have done so much better as a son. And those were the most difficult truths of all.

"My father wasn't looking to form a love connection through marriage, either," he said at last, the gentle pressure of Emily's fingertips prodding him to keep going. Lulling him, once again, into the sense he could trust her. "He already had one. He and his secretary, a Mr. Collard, have been in love from the time he inherited Rosemead at the age of two-and-twenty."

Emily's hand stilled, and her lips parted. While her shock likely didn't match what his own had been, she must feel some surprise at the revelation. Yet instead of exclaiming over it, she kept her palm atop his hand like a soft weight as she anticipated the rest of the story. The part of it that made his insides raw.

"Maybe I would have seen it had I been more perceptive." He gave his head a small shake, silently chiding himself for how bloody *thoughtless* he'd been. "For over three decades, my father devoted himself to the role of viscount—to undertaking his duties so flawlessly—as all the while, he lived with the burden that he could never have the one thing he truly desired. At least, not beyond the occasional clandestine meeting that left him in fear of what would happen if he and his secretary were discovered. Why I assumed his misery came from some curse surrounding Rosemead or the viscountcy, I haven't the faintest idea. The problem was never with the estate or the title itself. It was with his circumstances, which were made so much worse by having an ingrate heir who abandoned him. Who left all the responsibility to fall on his shoulders, so he felt like he could never escape."

"Oh, Nate ..." Finally, she spoke, her voice a soft murmur in the stillness, her fingers gently squeezing his. "I'm so sorry for everything Lord Pembrook went through, more than I can say, and I understand your regret. Yet I'm certain he wouldn't want you to keep condemning yourself. You cannot change your past decisions, but you're working to choose differently in the present. That's all you can ask of yourself."

He exhaled, the motion tugging at the knots in his chest. Perhaps her mollifying words had merit. However, all he knew for certain was that he felt damn sorry, too. "At least his circumstances have finally changed for the better." The one thing in the whole miserable situation for which Nate could feel thankful. "The ending of the war gave him the opportunity to travel to France, where he cannot be persecuted for whom he loves. And so, in the summer, he put himself first for a change and took it. He and Collard have been in Paris together ever since, where they're happy. My father isn't merely pretending anymore."

"I'm so glad." She'd long since finished the task of spreading ointment, but her hand remained clasped with his, her lips curving just the slightest bit. Enough that he could envision what she'd look like if she smiled.

"So, you see why I had to return," he said, the space between his ribs aching with a mixture of bittersweet emotions that had no name. "My father didn't cast off his responsibilities to Rosemead lightly. If nothing else, I could assuage his guilt by coming back in his stead and seeing that the St. Stephen's Day party goes ahead as usual." He sighed, his gaze traveling a moment to the snow-streaked windows. "Although I'm questioning whether I have the ability to manage it successfully, or if everything I touch is destined to become tainted by failure."

"It isn't." She was leaning closer to him now. Near enough that he could detect the flutter of her dark lashes and the whisper of her breath before she spoke. "You're doing your best, and that's admirable. Not a failure at all."

He wanted to believe her. Wanted to think he could atone for his years of disregard and become the future viscount that Rosemead needed. Yet his efforts since returning had been marked by setbacks, one after another, as if the universe insisted on punishing him. On refusing to let him forget the past.

Indeed, how *could* he forget the way he'd neglected his father?

Furthermore ... he now held the knowledge that in the midst of his youthful carelessness, he'd also neglected and hurt *her*.

"Emily, I ..." He wished he had the right words to express his remorse, his admiration, his fears, his desires. To let her know he trusted and valued her, and that if by some miracle he executed a successful party, he would have her to thank. He wished he could tell her how beautiful she looked in the dimming light with her tumbling braid and lips that brought to mind a blossoming rose. How his blood seemed to ignite whenever she was near.

But he didn't have those words, only had her beside him holding his hand, breathing the same air he did, peering at him with eyes of pure, bright amber.

And so, he acted instead.

He kissed her.

9

As a girl, Emily had often imagined the way Nate's lips would feel if they fell upon hers. She'd spent more time than she cared to admit pondering whether they'd be smooth or rough, whether they'd brush against her in a featherlight caress or overtake her with a consuming pressure.

However, her imaginings couldn't have prepared her for the way his kiss would steal the air from her lungs and make her heart detonate as if composed of fireworks. She couldn't have predicted that his lips themselves would be soft, but that the stubble along his jawline would lightly abrade her skin.

He neither skirted her lips nor ravished them, but pressed against them with a steady force, like he wished to savor her. To *know* her.

This was all a terrible idea. Something that shouldn't happen, *couldn't* happen, for it was a dream she'd long since thrown away. She'd learned her lesson, knew better than to return to childish fantasies.

And still, she didn't pull away. Didn't think about wisdom or old hurts or guarding her heart. Instead, she returned the pressure of his lips, allowing herself to know him, too.

As if of their own volition, her arms reached up to wrap around his neck, her fingers extending to comb through the hair that had grown long enough to curl at his nape. She'd long wondered what those dark gold strands would feel like, and it turned out they were sleek beneath her fingertips, something she could relish until dusk became dawn.

His hands, meanwhile, slid down her back to encircle her waist in a pleasurable embrace. Those battered hands that she'd held, stroked, and soothed as he laid bare all his secrets and regrets. As, little by little, he became less the young man who'd so flippantly dashed her feelings for him and more someone who'd matured, changed—someone to whom she wanted to give all her care and comfort.

But the longer their lips stayed connected, the less she could focus on who he'd been in the past or who he meant to be in the future. She could think only of how his tongue gently teased her until her mouth fell open, and of the hot jolt of bliss as the tip of his tongue flicked over hers.

She'd allowed gentlemen to kiss her before, but it had never been like this. She'd never had a man caress her lower back and experienced the sensation deep in her core, had never tasted another man's mouth so intimately and felt desire spiral in myriad directions. This wasn't a mild sensation that skirted the edge of enjoyment. This was champagne and butterflies, and she wanted more of it, wanted to become drunk and dizzy—

A sharp clatter echoed off the marble floor tiles, followed by a woman's startled gasp.

Something fell ... Someone's here ...

All at once, her brain made sense of the noises, and her body snapped to alertness, jerking away from him and sitting straight against the chair back.

The housekeeper, Mrs. Ruck, stood in the doorway

nearest the servant's stairs, holding a tray containing a teapot and an assortment of dishes and utensils. Minus one spoon, which had relocated to the floor below.

"I beg your pardon, sir. Lady Emily." After a moment of open-mouthed silence, the housekeeper managed a small curtsey, her cheeks turning a vibrant shade of crimson. "I found some more ointment in the stillroom and brought it along in case you have need of it, and Mrs. White thought you could both use some tea and biscuits. She also asked if you'd like dinner prepared and sent up. Although perhaps I'd best come back later—"

"No." Emily and Nate spoke in unison, and Nate beckoned Mrs. Ruck forward, pushing aside the basin so she could place the tray on the table in front of him.

The housekeeper was quick to obey, although she refused to quite look either of them in the eye. Not that Emily blamed her after the scene she'd witnessed. Emily swept a finger across her temple, her face feeling like it had been set afire.

As for Nate, he rummaged in his pocket for his watch. Glanced from the watch face to the windows with an expression that was strangely pinched. "Thank you," he said gruffly. Breathlessly. "We'll have dinner, although there's no need to prepare anything special or bring it to the dining room. We can go down to the kitchen instead. If that's agreeable to you, Lady Emily?"

Her heart seemed to have lost control, galloping like a horse free from its reins. Her stomach flipped and twisted, so the last thing she wanted was food. Yet what else was she to do or say? "Certainly." She jumped up from her chair, sucking in a quick mouthful of air that had grown charged and heavy. Her eyes darted around the great hall—the space she'd been familiar with for years but that suddenly looked foreign—and registered it was growing dark yet again.

Somehow, the hours of Christmas Eve had slipped by with her staring at neither the clock nor the elements. Almost as if she were meant to be at Rosemead and this wasn't all an unfortunate twist of fate.

She hurried away before the idea could blossom, stopping beside one of the towering windows with its frosty panes of glass. Sure enough, snow continued to drop relentlessly from the blackening sky, the wind swirling it about over the frozen landscape.

Yet the spiraling flakes outdoors couldn't compare to the whirlwind that had become her thoughts.

She and Nate didn't talk much over their simple meal of bread, cheese, and gingerbread biscuits.

Fortunately, Mrs. Ruck—recovered from her earlier shock —and Mrs. White were in the kitchen with them to fill the silence, exclaiming over how well the food preparations were coming along.

Emily—who'd become especially skilled at concealing her true emotions since her entrapment at Rosemead—offered a pleasant remark as much as she was able. After all, she agreed that they'd accomplished an impressive amount with their limited resources, and the entire household deserved to feel proud. She hoped, with an unexpected sort of fervor, that Nate thought so as well.

He seemed to, when he did make a comment. But mostly, he was quiet. Pensive.

Did he regret their kiss? Regret what he'd told her? She found herself repeatedly shooting glances his way, wishing she could see inside his head. But while her family often commented on her perceptiveness, she regrettably lacked the ability to decipher what lay that far below the surface. Especially with him.

He'd become a puzzle. For he was both the man who'd hurt her and the man who'd been running from his own fears and misgivings.

The man who was careless. The man who wished to make amends.

The man whom she wanted never to see again. The man whose kiss wouldn't stop running through her memory, making her body cry out for more.

She took a drink of the cider Mrs. White had poured for them, washing down the crumbs that stuck in her throat. Full darkness had long since fallen, brightened only by the drifting snow. Which inevitably meant another night at Rosemead, and she didn't know what to do with that. What to say. How to feel.

"Will you come with me to the great hall, Lady Emily?" At last, Nate turned to her, his low voice pulling her out of her thoughts.

She could still picture him standing above her chair by the kitchen hearth and asking the same question yesterday. Could remember her aloofness, her despondency, her resistance. How had so much changed in such a short time? How had she come to see him so differently?

She rose from her fireside chair without protest, trying to ignore the rapid thrum of her heart. And when he offered his arm, she took it, even though she was no longer certain whether he meant it simply as a polite gesture or as something more. Nor could she say which of those options she preferred.

She tried to push it from her mind, focusing instead on Nate's words as he bid his housekeeper and cook good night and issued the order that they, along with the rest of the sparse household staff, were to take the remainder of the evening off. Once she uttered her own farewells and they retreated into the corridor, though, the quiet made her thoughts race backward again, to when he'd led her from the kitchen and up the stairs the afternoon before. That brief period when his footfalls had been light and assured, and he'd nearly looked joyful, and she hadn't been sure whether she loathed him for it or felt something else entirely.

His carefree confidence was gone now, for his face had grown sober, and his steps were almost tentative. However, their path remained the same. Up the servant's staircase, along the narrow corridor, through the door that opened to the splendor of the great hall. And then, he motioned to the very place he had yesterday: the unlit fireplace, where the yule log had been rolled in, ready to be set aflame and mark the festive season.

"It's Christmas Eve." He took a few steps into the room, then glanced back at her with a newfound hesitance. "I thought we could light it, if you like."

She hovered by the doorway, peering at the sturdy piece of ash wood. The tree, of all things, that had set this whole misadventure in motion. Perhaps Nate was recalling how unkindly she'd taken his suggestion the first time he made it— the moment when the truth had sunk in that she was snowbound.

Yet everything was altered now. The great hall had been transformed, the jumble of tables and chairs arranged in neat rows, the gift baskets lined up and waiting, the tangled pile of greenery hung cheerily about the room.

And with it, something inside her had transformed, too. A part of her that no longer cursed the snow and her terrible luck. That no longer wanted to flee.

Her throat felt thick, and she swallowed, quietly crossing the room until she stood beside the fireplace. "Yes, I would like that. Very much."

He moved faster, then, coming up alongside her and

reaching for something tucked behind the holly bough upon the mantelpiece. Two scraps of wood, slightly charred around the edges. "These are from last year's yule log, apparently. Mrs. Ruck provided them." He lifted the splinters to the sconce beside the mantel, waiting until the flames from the candles took hold of the ends and extending one of the glowing shards to her. "Will you do the honors? It's only fitting."

Her fingers brushed against his as she accepted the offering, and while she'd spent more of the day than she could have imagined with their hands entwined, the sensation didn't fail to send a tingle over her skin. She knelt upon the cold marble, her eyes fixed on the flame. And then, she lowered her hand so the flame touched the ash bark, holding it there until the fire caught.

Yes, she supposed this was a fitting conclusion to Christmas Eve. Proof that their struggle in the woods hadn't been in vain.

His trousers made the faintest rustling noise as he lowered himself beside her, setting his flame to the other end of the yule log. More fire sparked, the glow gradually spreading until it became the beginnings of a blaze not easily extinguished. She turned her head, watching the light of it dance across his profile, displaying the sharp angles of his jaw, the gold of his brows, the straight line of his mouth. For a moment, everything was quiet except for the crackle of the yule log beneath the flames. Until all at once, his words came, mingling with the soft sounds of the fire. "Thank you, Lady Emily."

Oh, her heart was acting peculiar, leaping and quivering in a way it had no business doing from a simple expression of gratitude. She couldn't help it; she kept going back to the press of his lips, the weight of his arms around her, the warmth of his hands beneath hers. All the instances when she'd no longer felt like a foolish girl stuck in the wrong place at the wrong time but a woman to be desired. A woman he esteemed enough to trust.

"It was my pleasure, Mr. Pembrook," she said, her voice little more than a murmur. It was a wonder she remembered how to speak at all, for the light tang of wood smoke, the firelight, and the sheer closeness of him seemed to be interfering with her ability to form coherent thoughts. Yet she remained sentient enough to notice he looked solemn. To guess at what weighed on him and recognize what he needed to hear. "You're going to do your father proud."

His lips quirked the slightest bit before straightening, and she detected the subtle rush of his exhale, almost like a sigh. "I hope so..." He continued staring into the fire, his expression making him appear miles away. Silence fell again, save for the gentle crack of wood, and the heaviness of it stretched between them until a shower of sparks flared to life with a loud pop. A muscle in his jaw twitched, his fingers curling against the leg of his trousers. And then, there were more words, spoken in a tight rasp. "I'm sorry I couldn't bring you home today as I promised."

Her heart gave a tiny lurch. Was that truly what troubled him? He worried he'd let her down? She supposed he had every reason to think so. After all, she'd sat in his kitchen yesterday with her chattering teeth and broken boot, demanding to return to Beaumont.

But that was before, not now.

Not now.

She didn't have all the correct, careful words to explain herself. Wasn't sure if the correct words even existed. And so, she simply said what was in her heart. "Perhaps I'm already spending Christmas Eve where I'm meant to be."

His head pivoted so his gray eyes were no longer staring at worlds within the flames but at her. Firelight danced within his pupils. A vee formed at the bridge of his nose. And then, a lone fingertip reached up to trace along her cheek. To push a stray lock of hair behind her ear.

"Emily ..." Her name on his lips was a question. A plea.

"Nate," she whispered back, her pulse thundering, and she didn't know what else to say. Only knew what she wanted.

He'd leaned in and kissed her. Why could she not do the same and kiss him, too?

10

For a split second after her lips landed upon Nate's, he was very still. A split second when Emily questioned whether she'd been too hasty, if she'd misunderstood—

Except then, his arms shot around her waist, pulling her close, and his lips consumed her with a heated pressure that sent a flood of warmth shooting through her core. Their first kiss had begun with a sort of tenderness as they'd adjusted to the novel sensation of each other's mouths. However, this kiss was harder, urgent, and his fingers sank into her flesh like he never wished to release her.

She let her hands fall back around his nape, into his hair. Let him nudge her lips apart so their tongues could twine. Everything about him was hot. His breath, his touch, his body. It all made her feel as if she could burst into flames.

She gave a little cry as she felt her body being shifted, and suddenly, he sat on the floor with her atop his lap, her legs hanging to either side of his thighs. Oh, this was heavenly. Rather like being in his arms when he'd carried her through the snow, except this time, she could yield to the rigid muscles of his chest instead of fighting him. Plus, she had the added benefit of his thighs beneath her, the heat of them searing her. The hardness in his trousers brushing against her, alerting her of his desire. Making her own desire flare like the sparks within the fireplace.

"Emily," he breathed, his lips pulling away to skirt her jawline. Her neck. Traveling downward, little by little, and bringing so much promise. Yet he stopped his path to hover above her collarbone, peering up at her with a look that was part wide and desirous, part questioning.

"Please," she moaned, tilting her head, arching her back. How had her simple day gown suddenly grown too tight? The fabric too heavy? Her shift had become a burden; her stays would drive her mad.

But then, his fingers were at her back, loosening the tapes of her gown and laces of her stays. Her bodice drooped, and as it did, he lowered his mouth to the curve of her breast. Down to the nipple, covered only by her flimsy shift, that had grown taut and aching.

She cried out again, the sensation of his lips against the hardened bud making pleasure rush through her veins and yearning pool between her legs. He was relentless—licking, suckling, laving her through the fabric, first on one side and then the other, until she didn't know whether to consider it bliss or torture. The sensation was good, *so* good, but it wasn't enough, and she grew desperate, needy—

Until all at once, he was lifting her, and they were no longer on the floor but standing on shaky feet. It was fortunate he kept her clasped tightly against him, for desire had rendered her knees weak, and were he to let go, she wasn't confident she'd remain upright.

But he didn't let go. Instead, he claimed her lips again, guiding her backward until her legs collided with something solid. *The dining table.*

No sooner did her mind make the connection than he was

grasping her hips, boosting her onto the tabletop, causing the decorative holly bough in the center to tumble to the floor with a single long sweep of his arm.

The air rushed from her lungs, the sound of her gasp getting swallowed by his kiss. As if by instinct, her legs fell open, and he leaned into her, his arousal hot and tempting between her thighs. Some rational spark within her brain tried to warn her that they were ruining the decorations, that a servant could walk in, that nothing about this was wise. However, she couldn't make herself care. Couldn't focus on anything but thoughts of pulling up her skirts, unfastening his trousers, and feeling the hardness of his manhood deep inside her.

All until he tore his lips away and pressed his forehead to hers, his breath coming in ragged pants. "I won't compromise you." His voice had turned guttural.

She blinked, trying to make sense of the maelstrom of sensations that twisted her in knots. He was correct, of course. She shouldn't desire such a thing, would do far better to walk away before they crossed a dangerous line. She *knew* that. Regardless, it didn't stop the sting of disappointment or the protest in each of her nerve endings, because she craved so deeply, she *needed*—

"But that doesn't mean I cannot give you pleasure." His words caused a jolt low in her belly, and her unsatiated body snapped to alertness. "Let me see you." His hand left her hip, his index finger trailing down the fabric covering her thigh. Moving in time to his rough, heated murmur. "Let. Me. Taste. You."

Her mouth fell open at his wicked proposal, and a breathy sound escaped her lips. Was it a cry of shock? Of desire? Either way, the cry turned into a single intelligible word. "Yes."

Yes. He sank to his knees before her and peered upward, the glint in his eyes holding so much promise.

Yes. He bunched up her skirts until they formed a heap on the tabletop, uttering a throaty command for her to hold them.

Yes, yes, yes. Perhaps she should be ashamed of sitting on a table in front of him like this, so bare and exposed. Yet he continued staring at her with pupils huge with longing, drawing close enough that his breath tickled her sensitive flesh, and she could only think of how badly she wanted.

His tongue swept a long circle over her sex, and she jerked against the table, the pleasure of it causing stars to shoot across her vision.

"Do you like that, love?" His tongue retreated, hovering just above where she longed for it, and the hot trickle of air from his words nearly drove her mad. "You're exquisitely sweet, you know."

"Mm." Suddenly, even *yes* had become too much for her; all she had left was a breathless moan.

A moan that enticed him to take hold of her hips and tug them forward. To push her legs even farther apart and drape them over his shoulders so he could see every secret part of her. To grin roguishly as if he were about to enjoy the dessert course.

And then, he feasted on her without relenting, licking and sucking at her folds. Moving up to the little peak that contained the heart of her pleasure.

She dropped back on her elbow, her hand continuing to clamp tight to the swaths of green muslin around her waist. Her other hand shooting out and scrabbling clumsily until she grasped a fistful of his hair, anchoring him close to her. If he were to pull away now, she may very well die from it.

But he didn't pull away; he drew her pearl between his lips, his caresses becoming more intense. Her body was so taut, so close to hurtling over a cliff and into a shower of euphoria. She screwed her eyes shut, her hips undulating beyond her control, her muscles quivering, her fingernails sinking into his scalp.

And suddenly, there came a new sensation—a sturdy finger dipping into the wetness at her entrance, gently circling the untried flesh.

Release washed over her like a deluge, making her come apart with spasm after spasm of pleasure. Nothing she'd done at night in the solitude of her bedchamber could have prepared her for anything this intense, this all-consuming. And he stayed with her for it all, fastidiously lapping at her sex, drawing out each blissful wave until her body was spent.

When she opened her eyes, the room appeared to have transformed again. Not because anything was outwardly altered—aside from the tabletop holly bough that now lay on the floor—but because her senses felt like they'd sharpened. As if the firelight grew brighter, the evergreen branches more fragrant, the heat of Nate's body more intense.

She gave his hair a soft tug, and he pushed onto his feet, pulling her back up to sitting and into his arms, claiming her lips in a fervent kiss. His mouth tasted different, muskier. Like *her*, she realized, her intimate muscles giving another twitch. She let her bunched-up skirts drop, finally allowing herself the privilege of sliding her hand down his chest, exploring the firm ridges that were apparent even through his shirt and waistcoat. Continuing lower until she reached the thick wool of his trousers and the hardness that tented them in the front, curling her fingers around the bulge.

He let out a groan, his body tensing as if he were in pain. She stilled her hands, breaking away from the kiss so she could peer at him, a crease forming in her brow. "Did I do something wrong?"

"No. You're perfect. What's wrong," he said between clenched teeth, "is that you'll unman me."

Oh. Desire unfurled in her belly like plumes of smoke.

Not for what her own body craved, but for the pleasure she wished to give to him. So she could see him desperate and unhinged.

She hopped to the floor, using her foot to hook the nearest chair leg and drag it out from under the table. "Let me." She glanced at the seat, then laid her palms against his chest and nudged him toward it. The size of her body was no match for his. Regardless, he toppled into the chair like his legs had become boneless. "I want to touch you."

"Emily." He didn't speak so much as growl her name as she got to her knees in front of him. Positioning herself the same way he'd done right before he'd set her yearning alight. "Do you have any idea how much I desire you?"

Those words. The things they did to her pulse. To the very center of her. "Then let me have you," she said, her voice mostly breath.

Her fingers went to the top buttons of his fall, slipping them from their holes. She worked her way downward, watching intently as the fabric began to gape, until at last, there were no buttons left and his arousal sprang free.

She'd thought she knew what to expect. She'd seen statues of unclothed men, after all, along with a few illustrated books on the highest shelves of the Beaumont library that weren't intended for her eyes. However, none of that prepared her for how swollen and large Nate would look in real life. How very rigid and hot he would feel when she lightly set her fingertips around his girth.

She gave him a careful caress from base to tip, and when his breath hitched, she did it again, studying his face for his reaction.

His mouth was slack, his eyelids heavy as he peered back at her. "That's it, love. So good." His hand fell atop hers, squeezing her fingers tighter around him, guiding her up his length in one powerful stroke. "You can press harder, like this," he muttered, his voice sounding on the verge of crack-ing. "It feels so good when you ..."

His words became a harsh gasp as she repeated the motion several times in rapid succession. And because his head was tilted back, his features twisting in pleasure, she kept going, pumping her hand over the velvety skin that was steel under-neath. A bead of dew appeared at the tip of his erection, and she slid her fingers over it, loving the slippery hardness of him, the quivering of his thighs, the raggedness of his inhales and exhales—all because of *her* ministrations.

Yet she wanted to both give and take even more from him. Wanted to know him as intimately as he knew her.

She leaned forward, swirling her tongue over the thick head of his arousal.

"Jesus, Emily," he hissed, his hips jolting against the seat, his hand shooting out to clutch her braid

She almost halted to pull away and ask once again if she'd erred. Except she knew better now, didn't she? The problem wasn't that the sensation displeased him but that it drove him out of his head with need.

Which was exactly as she wished it.

She licked the salt of his skin, pressed tiny kisses up and down his shaft as her hand continued to stroke. And then, she dared to do something she'd seen in one of the illicit library books: she took the crown of his manhood between her lips and drew him into her mouth.

When he groaned her name this time, it came out stran-gled and distorted. His whole body shuddered, and she repeated the motion once, twice—

"Enough, I'm going to—" He wrenched himself away from her lips, his hand flying down to encapsulate hers, giving a powerful thrust that brought on his release. She watched in fascination while he came undone, feeling him pulse beneath her touch as his seed spilled upon the floor.

Until his limbs, like hers, became loose and sated in the aftermath of pleasure.

She'd never felt so powerful. Had never imagined a sensation like this, for champagne and butterflies didn't begin to express its potency.

He made quick work of retrieving a handkerchief from his pocket and cleaning the evidence of their lovemaking away, after which he lured her upward, pulling her onto his lap. Without another thought, she sank against his chest and rested her face in the crook of his neck. He was so solid and warm. He simply felt *right*.

His mouth came down to brush along the hair near her temple. "Good God, my lady." His breath was hot, delicious. "What you do to me."

Her lips quirked, and a muscle clenched low in her abdomen. *What you do to me, too, Nate.*

She let him hold her close and rub her shoulders and back. Let him whisper flattering words in her ear about how beautiful she was, and she basked in them, as languid as one of her pet cats. All until he eventually returned to the laces and tapes he'd unfastened and retied them, carefully setting her stays and bodice back to rights.

The moment had to come sooner or later. She knew that, and she made herself shift on his lap so she could return the favor, sliding each button of his fall into place. However, that didn't stop her stomach from doing an odd flip.

Intimacy had made her powerful, but it rendered her vulnerable, too. Because what came next? As long as they remained in the great hall, she had firelight, warmth, the leftover haze of her pleasure, the safety of Nate's embrace. Yet it was like a bubble, ready to burst. For as soon as she climbed the stairs to her borrowed bedchamber, there would be only coldness. The return of darkness. And something that was perhaps even worse—her pounding, conflicted heart, keeping her up all night as it swelled with emotions she shouldn't let herself acknowledge.

"Do you think ..." She hesitated, her throat suddenly dry. Her eyes no longer willing to quite lock with his. She didn't want to be weak and needy, didn't want to be *childish*. Except ... what if she could trust him not to see her that way anymore? What if she could allow herself to be open with him and know he would give her a safe place to fall?

She swallowed, then permitted the question to break free. "Do you think you could sit with me by the fire for a little while longer?"

Right away, his hand went out to cup her chin, coaxing her to look at him, and her chest clenched in anticipation. There was no condescension in his expression. In fact, he was observing her rather like she held the stars and moon. "Of course, love." He traced a path along her jawline and brushed a stray strand of hair away from her cheek. "Just give me one moment. I'll return directly."

He gently lifted her from his lap and rose, flashing her a lazy half-smile before he hurried out of the great hall and disappeared behind one of the doors. A smile that made her insides warm, until her lips nearly curved upward as well.

This night would end, but not yet. *Not yet.*

True to his word, he returned to the great hall without delay, his arms laden with a stack of blankets and two plump cushions. "We may as well enjoy the fire in comfort."

She could think of nothing in this moment that sounded better.

She scurried over to him, taking the opposite side of the heavy wool blanket and helping to spread it into a perfect rectangle against the floor. Then, she placed the cushions at the farthest end from the fireplace while he set another folded blanket to the side of them.

He motioned for her to sit, and she readily complied,

kicking off her slippers and sinking onto the soft surface. Letting herself recline against a cushion so she faced the fire, which had developed into a healthy blaze.

He lowered himself as well, sitting on the edge of the blanket while he removed his boots and then shuffling over to stretch out beside her. Draping a protective arm across her abdomen.

A wind gust rattled the windowpanes as if to remind her of the storm's existence, but suddenly, it didn't matter. Nothing mattered of the outside world, of the weather, of the past or future. Nothing mattered at all beyond the two of them in this makeshift bed beneath the yule log's warm glow.

For endless minutes, she watched the flames dance in the fireplace. Alternated with watching the shadows they cast across his face. Neither she nor Nate attempted speech; it simply didn't seem necessary. The crackle of wood—and the closeness they shared—was enough.

Eventually, her eyelids grew heavy, and exhaustion began closing in on her. A sure sign the time had come to retreat to her bed. Yet he didn't move from the blanket, and so, neither did she. She didn't seem to have the energy. Or the will.

Instead, she let her eyes close, giving in to the warmth and lightness that overtook her body. She became vaguely aware of a quiet shuffling beside her, and then, the soft weight of another blanket falling upon her, topped again by Nate's strong arm.

She threaded her fingers through his and rolled onto her side, and he followed, his chest cradling her back, keeping her warm. Sheltered. For a fraction of a moment, her eyes drifted open, taking a blurry look at her surroundings before sleep came to pull her under.

Too brief a time for her to fully register that beyond the windows, the snow had stopped.

11

Nate's sleep-hazed brain knew nothing but contentment. Nothing but warmth, and softness, and a sweet, rich fragrance that acted upon his senses like an elixir.

There was a weight in his arms. A body curled against his. *Emily.* Fragments of memories began to materialize, and he smiled as they drifted through his head. Emily on the dining table, crying out in pleasure as he knelt between her thighs and savored that glorious quim. Emily with her lips upon his cock, stroking him until he came harder than he ever had in his life. Emily falling asleep beside him in front of the fire, her face soft and tranquil in the low light.

But something was wrong. There was no more darkness, no more subtle sway of firelight. A strange illumination pierced his eyelids, and something pounded against the floor. He could almost swear someone called his name ...

His eyelids flew open, and he blinked rapidly, trying to make sense of surroundings that no longer felt right. He was still in the great hall, to be sure. However, the space had turned bright.

Flooded by sunlight.

He bolted up to sitting, his blurry gaze falling upon thick gray skirts hovering at his side. Which made him promptly turn his eyes upward, where he was met with the frantic countenance of Mrs. Ruck.

"Mr. Pembrook." She wrung her hands together, her brow puckering anxiously. "Lord Rockliffe has just arrived."

Lord Rockliffe ... The name took a second or two to solidify within his mind. A second or two before his stomach sank to his toes, and he turned abruptly, ready to nudge Emily awake.

However, she was already sitting, staring at him in wide-eyed alarm. And then, she was on her feet, cramming slippers over her stockings while simultaneously giving her crumpled dress a few tugs.

The torrent rushing through his head was half dread, half sluggish disbelief. Nonetheless, he managed to vault from the blanket and drag a hand over his unruly hair. To hastily smooth his waistcoat and shove the boots back on his feet. All until it occurred to him that the bed on the floor presented the more pressing issue.

He swept the blankets and pillows into his arms, running to the servant's door and heaving the bundle inside.

Just in time, for the moment he slammed that door closed again, the main doors burst open, and there was Lord Rockliffe, striding briskly into the room, his mouth set in a grim line.

Emily had been quick enough to dart to the table they'd left in disarray and retrieve the discarded holly bough, and she worked to straighten it in the center of the tabletop. However, she abandoned the holly the instant her eyes fell upon her father, and she sprinted forward, crashing into his chest and wrapping him in an embrace. "Papa! I'm so happy to see you."

The marquess's features softened at once, and he pulled

her tight against his greatcoat. "You, too, Em. You cannot imagine how much. We were all worried about you."

She released her grip on him and stood back, her mouth twisting into a frown. "But Joseph—"

"Told us what happened, yes." Lord Rockliffe's eyes did a quick scan of the room, and he seemed to notice Nate's presence for the first time—although what he thought of his discovery remained indecipherable. "That couldn't stop us from feeling uneasy until we had you home safe where you belong. All the footmen and grooms have been helping to clear snow since dawn, and we were finally able to get the sleigh through, thank God."

Nate shifted warily, a cloying heat spreading over the back of his neck and up to his ears. Everyone at Beaumont had been toiling away to reestablish a path between there and Rosemead, which was what he *should* have been doing the minute the snow stopped. Instead, he'd broken his commitment to seeing her home safely in favor of lazing about, holding her tight to him like a thief in possession of a stolen gem, until the stormy night faded and gleaming sunrays streaked through the windows. Brilliant enough to expose all his failings.

For another fleeting moment, Lord Rockliffe's ice blue eyes fell upon him before flicking back to Emily. This time, though, his countenance didn't soften, and he set his hands on her shoulders, looking her up and down. "Are you well?"

"Yes, of course." She gave a tight smile, and if Nate could notice that her voice sounded a touch higher than usual, her father must recognize it, too. "Mr. Pembrook was a fine host, and I was able to help him with the preparations for his St. Stephen's Day party while the snow kept us trapped."

"Indeed." The marquess abruptly concluded his assessment, and when his attention shot to Nate this time, it stuck. Lord Rockliffe nodded in acknowledgment, although the gesture didn't have the air of a friendly greeting. Not that he looked angry, exactly, as much as his mien was large and imposing. Rather, he seemed to be contemplating, like he wasn't quite certain what he'd walked in on but was determined to solve the puzzle.

Another damnable surge of warmth flooded Nate's skin. Lord Rockliffe's narrowed eyes were so intense that he could almost believe the marquess *would* discern the truth if only he kept staring long enough. That the sunrays would illuminate the place on the floor where the temporary bed had laid, and he'd *know* why Emily hadn't come home earlier in the morning.

After which the Marquess of Rockliffe would rightly murder him on the spot, and Nate wouldn't even regret it, for he'd consider it a fair price to pay for having Emily all for his own, even if he'd been granted the privilege merely for one night.

But suddenly, the large double doors flew open again, and the marquess's powerful stare broke away, turning to the man who hovered in the doorway. The young man with a fashionable top hat, smartly cut greatcoat, and polished boots dusted with a layer of snow. The man whose gaze immediately went to Emily, and Nate recognized the stranger at once without anyone saying a word.

She whirled unsteadily to face the door, but if the sight of whom she encountered there caused her insides to freeze with shock, it showed upon her features no more than a half-second before she regained the tiny smile that didn't meet her eyes and started forward to greet him. "Lord Coleville."

That was the moment when Nate experienced a true pommel of regret crashing into his abdomen. Regret, and bitterness, and a harsh, sickening lurch that could be nothing but jealousy. He wasn't sure what he'd envisioned when Emily had mentioned her *almost* betrothed. Perhaps someone wizened and cantankerous instead of a spirited young earl with aristocratic good looks and an eager smile? Or perhaps he'd never considered the other man much at all, because for as long as the snow fell, she'd felt like *his*.

She didn't crash into the earl's arms the way she'd done with her father. *She doesn't love him.* But the idea brought Nate no comfort. Lord Coleville lifted Emily's hand to his lips and kissed it, and Nate couldn't feel anything other than a deep, covetous ache.

"I apologize for not being at Beaumont to welcome you when you arrived." Emily peered into the earl's dark, vibrant eyes, her tone a perfect blend of pleasantness and composure. "How fortunate that your travels weren't impeded by the weather."

"I reached Beaumont Manor right before the roads became impassable." Lord Coleville was equally composed, blast him, in this happy reunion with his future betrothed. Equally pleasant. "But the real good fortune is that the sun came out and we were able to reach you in time for Christmas Day."

"I'm so grateful." Her expression didn't change drastically but wavered just the slightest amount, and her eyes shifted to the side. Toward where Nate lingered by the servant's door, as if she suddenly remembered his presence. "Rest assured, I stayed well and was given every comfort while snowbound."

She took an audible breath, her arm stiff as she gestured to Nate. "Lord Coleville, may I introduce my host, and the gentleman who was kind enough to offer me shelter throughout the storm, Mr. Nathaniel Pembrook."

She said his name so blandly, as if she'd never been carried in his arms, had never shared her secrets with him in the middle of the night, had never lain on the table while he learned every intimate fold of her.

With great effort, Nate returned the earl's cordial bow. He

knew so little of the man, but Lord Coleville's position alone —not as a peer, but as the future husband of Lady Emily Prescott—made Nate despise him.

Although that was hardly fair, was it? His fingers clenched, his injured hand giving a throb of protest. Instead of begrudging Lord Coleville for having what he could not, he'd be wiser to point an accusatory finger in his own direction. Because *he* was the one who'd been shortsighted and selfish; *he* was the one who'd run away; *he* was the one who'd wasted an opportunity and let someone so magnificent slip from his grasp.

"On that note, we should be on our way again before the whole Prescott family takes it in mind to come help with the rescue effort." Lord Rockliffe's declaration swiftly pulled Nate from his spiraling thoughts, and the marquess turned to him with another nod. No longer suspicious but affable. "I thank you, Pembrook, for extending your hospitality to my daughter. If you have no other plans, Lady Rockliffe and I would welcome you to our table this evening so you can partake of Christmas dinner with us."

The yule log burned heartily, but Nate's blood had turned to ice. For a flash of a moment, it sounded wonderful: sitting around a table filled with Prescotts just like on Christmases past, as if he were being given another chance to appreciate what he hadn't back then.

Yet it wouldn't negate everything that had changed. Namely, that Emily would sit across the table from him with her intended, and instead of feeling indifferent, Nate would find the force of his longing—his envy—gnawing through his gut. God, what if Coleville decided that the dinner table made the ideal location to propose?

He tensed his shoulders, trying to appear as composed as Lady Emily and her perfect earl. Knowing he didn't succeed. "I appreciate the invitation, but I'm afraid I must decline.

There are still some preparations for the fete tomorrow that I need to oversee."

Lord Rockliffe cocked his head, almost like he was of a mind to argue. Just as quickly, though, he straightened again with a curt dip of his chin. "As you wish. Now that we've cleared a path, we'll see that the roast geese are sent over to you as promised."

Nate's throat felt thick, coated with the bitterness of bile. And still, he managed to choke out words, as if everything in his world hadn't gone awry. "I thank you kindly."

Lord Rockliffe took that as his cue to start toward the large double doors, where Mrs. Ruck had silently appeared, holding out Emily's cloak and gloves. The earl followed, straightening his already flawless hat, no doubt assuming that Emily would remain at his side.

But she didn't. She moved in the opposite direction, toward Nate, and for one auspicious moment, his heart felt ready to explode out of his chest.

All until she arrived in front of him, leaving a respectable distance between their bodies, and folded herself into a practiced curtsey. "Thank you, Mr. Pembrook, for everything."

Damn it, he didn't want that decorous gesture. Those careful words. He wanted her in his arms, baring every intimate part of herself—body and soul—to him. He wanted her to stay at his side, always, because she allowed him to think that his role as heir and future viscount wasn't destined to end in failure.

She made Rosemead better. She made *him* better.

However, the weight of too many eyes rested upon them both, and he could give nothing in return but an equally polite reply. "It is I who must thank you for the assistance you provided."

"Of course." She was so reserved, so careful. That tiny

waver returned to her voice, though, and she bit down on her lip, her eyes locking with his. Not darting away.

What transpired beneath those liquid amber depths? The intensity of them pulled him in, potent enough to make the burden of all other gazes vanish. Nothing existed but her, and a voice cropped up in the back of his head. *Tell her.*

His fingers clenched tighter, heedless of the pain, for the voice was like a spark against tinder, bursting into flames. *Tell her you were an idiot all those years ago. Tell her you're not blind anymore. Tell her you've gotten so many things wrong, but that if she's willing to forgive your past offenses, you'll spend the rest of your life trying to be a better man. For your father, for the estate, and for her, because no one has ever made your heart yearn the way she has.*

He took a breath, fighting past the ache in his lungs, the bands around his chest.

But suddenly, she broke the stare, and something in her countenance shifted. Became shuttered. Perhaps she'd already seen everything she needed to see.

"Happy Christmas, Nate." Her words came out as a whisper for his ears only, containing a note he couldn't quite interpret. Was it sadness? Disappointment? Longing?

Or maybe it was none of those things; maybe he projected his own sentiments while, in truth, she intended nothing but an insignificant farewell. For she was walking away, toward her waiting cloak and her father. Toward her *almost* betrothed, who'd turned back to extend an arm to her.

Wait. Don't leave. Nate wanted to call out, to shout her name to the rafters. But to what purpose?

The snow had brought her to him and kept them ensconced until he'd started to believe in impossible things. However, the storm was over now. The sun had come out, and if it continued shining so brilliantly, the powerful rays would devour the blanket of white as if it had never been.

The rest of the world had returned. A world in which Emily had already forged a path forward and knew what she wanted from the future. His chance with her had already come and gone. Some mistakes couldn't be undone.

She was never mine to keep.

He stood as if made of stone, the throbbing in his hand no match for the pain clawing between his ribs. "Happy Christmas, Emily," he said, a murmur that was overshadowed by the sound of top boots beating against the marble floor tiles.

And then, he watched her go.

12

Emily had been absent from home for an unexpectedly long time, but she would never know it from the Beaumont Manor drawing room, which contained the same commotion she'd left behind two days prior. If anything, the chaos only intensified the instant she stepped through the doorway, for Anna spotted her right away, dropping the ball of yarn she'd been using to entertain their two cats and squealing her name in delight.

From there, Emily found herself showered with hugs and exclamations that all ran together in an enthusiastic jumble. Phoebe and her aunt Amelia both kissed her on the cheek. Her youngest cousins tugged at her skirts. Someone—her older cousin, Alexander, she believed—said something about getting her chocolate and gingerbread, and Christmas greetings came from all directions.

Emily let herself bask in her family's affection, and for a few happy seconds, she experienced nothing but fulfillment. A few seconds before the ache in her chest started again, and she didn't know whether she should throw back her head and laugh or sink to the floor and sob.

But there was time to do neither, for Anna clasped her hands, leading her to one of the plush sofas and pulling her down to sit. "We should give you your presents. None of us have exchanged any yet; we all waited for you. But I think you should be the first to receive them."

Emily squeezed her sister's hand, wishing she could match Anna's eagerness and wide grin. How was it possible to feel bright and joyful, and so utterly despondent, all at the same time?

"Indeed." Another voice joined the cacophony. The voice of the man who'd helped her father rescue her, who looked so handsome as he came toward the sofa in his finely tailored green coat and tan trousers. He gave Anna a grateful smile as she rose to offer him her spot, and he settled beside Emily, still smelling pleasingly of the crisp outdoors. "And perhaps I could have the privilege of being the first to present my gift to you."

Emily swallowed tightly, watching Lord Coleville rummage in his pocket until his hand emerged with a small box. She managed the necessary thanks, although her limbs were brittle as she accepted it. He was a good man: charming, sensible, and well-mannered. Why, then, did sitting this close to him evoke nothing more in her than a mild sense of appreciation?

The box contained a delicately engraved gold ring, adorned in the center by a cluster of diamonds and emeralds. She let out a small gasp as she lifted the extravagant piece of jewelry between her fingers, bringing it closer to her face so she could be sure she hadn't entered a dream. "It's beautiful. Thank you," she said, watching the diamonds glint beneath the sun.

It was the type of gift a gentleman would only give a lady if he had certain intentions toward her.

"I'm pleased you like it." Lord Coleville gently took the

ring from her grasp and slid it onto her finger, giving a satisfied nod at the gems that sparkled against her pale skin. "My gift comes with a question."

Her stomach dropped even before he lowered himself to one knee upon the carpet. Because she knew what was coming and knew, in her heart of hearts, it was wrong, but she also didn't know how to stop it. How to alter this path that *she* had encouraged, that she'd tried so hard to make the right one.

"Lady Emily Prescott." He looked up at her, his eyes warm and brown. His cheeks just the tiniest bit flushed—perhaps an aftereffect of the cold, perhaps a consequence of what he was about to ask. "Will you do me the honor of becoming my wife?"

The question echoed through the air, and then, there was nothing, for her family's boisterous chatter faded to silence. Everyone had heard the proposal. Everyone stood in perfect stillness, awaiting her response.

She couldn't help but let her eyes wander for an instant. To her youngest cousins, who looked ready to jump up and down with excitement. To her father and uncle Jonathan, who wished to make the earl their ally in Parliament. To her grandmother, who surveyed the scene with the sharp gaze of a hawk. And to Anna, who appeared so bright and eager, for she would soon have her own first Season on the marriage mart and staunchly believed in fairytales and happy endings.

Emily hastily restored her focus to Lord Coleville's kind eyes and keen half-smile. Any woman would be lucky to have him. And yet, what existed between them wasn't love. It might never *be* love, because love was an illusion, a rarity, something on which she couldn't rely.

Except her mind flashed back to Nate. The boy for whom she'd pinched her cheeks and styled her hair. The man whose injured hand she'd held and stroked as he shared his innermost secrets with her. The man who'd comforted her, too, when she'd been afraid and vulnerable. The man who'd drawn pleasure from every intimate piece of her until her body lay overwrought and trembling, and her heart quivered and leaped.

She shoved the memories away, wishing she could snuff them like a candle and they'd be forever vanquished.

That wasn't possible, of course. The memories may very well haunt her for the rest of her life. However, she would have to learn to live with them, to make them not matter. For there was only one answer she could give.

"Yes."

A wreath, of all things, proved Emily's downfall.

She was lounging on the sofa later that afternoon, with a steaming cup of tea in hand and her elderly ginger cat Marigold curled upon her lap, when the bits of greenery caught her eye. Not the cheery evergreen branches that had been hung about the room in her absence, but a few discarded scraps of holly and ribbon that were twisted into an untidy circle and cast upon an end table. Specifically, the scraps she'd been shaping into a festive wreath before frustration had driven her to a fateful walk in the woods.

Her poor attempt at a decoration must have been lying there the whole time. However, it wasn't until now, when most of her relatives had dispersed to other parts of the house and the room had quieted, that it drew her notice.

For some irrational, inexplicable reason, the sight made her throat thick.

"Why is this still here?" she choked out, setting her teacup down with an ungraceful clatter.

"Oh!" Anna, who was reading a novel in the armchair next to her, looked up in surprise, her gaze following Emily's to the seemingly innocuous decor. "No one wanted to touch it, for we thought you might like to finish it yourself. We were determined, you see, that you would be back at Beaumont in time for Christmas."

That was a reasonable explanation. A touching one, really.

One that promptly made Emily burst into tears.

"Emily!" Anna was on the sofa in an instant, her pale brows drawn in alarm. "Em, what is it? Because I think you've been altogether too hard on yourself regarding that wreath …"

She trailed off, her mouth dipping into a frown. Her forehead wrinkling in concentration. "But the wreath has never truly been the problem, has it?"

No, of course it wasn't. Well, not beyond the fact that Emily wasn't certain whether her act of bringing greenery in early had cursed her with the worst luck or led to the most blissful night of her life.

Anna—who was getting so mature, and rather perceptive for her seventeen years—leaned in to give her a quick hug before jumping to her feet. "Wait here a moment," she said. "I know just what you need."

Emily watched her sister scurry away through the haze of her tears, trying to blink back the moisture. However, it wouldn't dissipate. No matter how tautly she attempted to hold her spine, no matter how hard she tried soothing herself by stroking Marigold's silky fur, the rivers wouldn't cease pouring down her cheeks. Her chest wouldn't stop heaving with great, shuddering sobs.

What was *wrong* with her? She didn't know why she was acting this way, or how to make things right again. She didn't know anything anymore, besides the fact that if she didn't stop crying soon, Benedict and Alexander would return with Lord Coleville from their ice-skating venture, and everyone would witness her teary-eyed folly.

But even the threat of detection wouldn't make her tears

dry up. They consumed her, making her sniffle and hiccup, until a hand fell upon her shoulder.

She startled, her head whipping upward.

"Grandmother," she exclaimed on a quivery breath, taking in the crepey fingers that rested on her shoulder and then meeting the grooved face that stared down at her. The last she'd noticed, the dowager marchioness had been dozing on the sofa nearest the fireplace, and without the demanding ring of the dowager's bell, Emily supposed she'd forgotten about her presence in the drawing room.

However, the dowager was very much still here. Not only that, but she was upright, her diminished body resting heavily against her cane but looking regal, nonetheless. "The earl is a solid, sensible match," she said abruptly, her shrewd blue gaze making her appear as if she knew every thought in Emily's head. "But not the right one."

Emily's mouth slackened, and the sob racking her chest hitched and then vanished. She dragged her fingers over her cheeks in a few hasty swipes, her shoulders stiffening beneath her grandmother's cool touch and her widened eyes beginning to narrow.

Why would the dowager think it appropriate to say something so presumptuous? She was a cold woman, one who'd always held herself at a distance from anything so undignified as outward familial affection. Perhaps her instincts to interfere and meddle—put to disuse during her illness—were coming back stronger than ever, and Emily nearly offered the biting retort that she was sorely mistaken.

Except the dowager wasn't mistaken. She'd never been a kindly and doting grandmother, yet she saw the truth in her granddaughter's heart.

All at once, the fight drained from Emily's body, and she allowed her shoulders to slump against the sofa. Why put up a shield when she'd already displayed her weakness? Why utter words that her grandmother would recognize as a lie? She squeezed her eyes shut, the remnants of tears slipping out as she gave her head a subtle shake.

"The question is, what are you going to do about it?" The dowager's clipped tone made Emily snap back to alertness, and she found those hard, icy eyes staring at her more intently than ever.

"It's your choice, gel. But remember this." The dowager gave a brisk nod, then held her chin pointed proudly upright. For the old lady was frail but fierce. Never afraid to voice her opinions or go after what she wanted. "Prescotts do not cower."

Again, Emily's jaw loosened, and a sharp pang, almost like the tip of an arrow, hit her between the ribs.

But there was no time to recover from it, no time to let the words percolate, for her grandmother gave her cane a single tap against the floor, and two strapping footmen emerged out of nowhere to whisk her away.

Emily blinked at the doorway in bewilderment, the short encounter feeling almost like a fevered dream. However, no sooner did the trio depart than her father and stepmother appeared, rushing over to the sofa and positioning themselves on either side of her.

For a moment, no one spoke. There were simply arms around her shoulders, and eyes much gentler than the dowager's peering at her, and a choking lump rising in her throat once more.

Her gaze darted back and forth, moisture welling beneath her eyelids until she was certain she would cry again. The only thing she didn't know was whose shoulder to cry upon.

Ultimately, she shed tears on both. She let her parents rub her back and wipe her cheeks, just like when she was a child, and she didn't even try to fight it. She simply let the sobs come until her body was weary and raw, and she at last found the strength to lift her head. To meet their anxious gazes and pose a single question: "Why didn't you tell me he'd returned?"

The *he* to whom she referred must be obvious without further explanation, for Phoebe's brows shot up, and her lips parted.

As for her father, a thundercloud passed over his features, and his voice became a dangerous rasp. "If Pembrook did something to hurt you, Em, then so help me God—"

"He didn't." She shook her head firmly, quashing the suggestion before it could take hold. Because Nate hadn't hurt her, not in the way her father must be imagining. On the contrary, he'd brought her to life, making her care and crave and soar in ways she hadn't before. The only thing hurting was her bruised, conflicted heart.

"Emily." Phoebe reached for her hand, gently clasping it within her own. "I never intended to keep secrets from you. Nor could anyone have anticipated the snowstorm or Mr. Pembrook's location when you set out on your walk. However ..." She hesitated a moment, letting out a quiet sigh. "You've avoided Rosemead for so long. As is your right, and your papa and I would never force you to do otherwise. Sometimes, though, one can better handle one's worries by confronting them rather than shying away."

Prescotts do not cower. Her grandmother's words came echoing back to her, causing a jolt within Emily's chest. As a girl of sixteen, she'd kept her heartache and humiliation locked deep inside her until everything became a jumbled mess and she no longer trusted her own feelings. However, her eyes were too swollen, her cheeks too wet, to hide them now.

And so, she pressed down on Phoebe's fingers, letting the long-ago secret slip from her tongue. "I used to fancy myself in love with him."

Phoebe pulled her stepdaughter close, her arm a

comforting weight around the back of Emily's neck. "I know," she murmured.

She ... she *knew*?

Yes. Of course she did. Emily let herself sink into the embrace, the air draining from her lungs in a wobbling exhale. She didn't know why she hadn't considered the possibility before, given that her girlish attempts to gain Nate's notice, followed by her long string of Christmas Eve illnesses, had been far from subtle. Certainly not above the notice of a concerned parent.

In a way, there was something comforting about having her hidden burden out in the open for her parents to share. However, that was only the small portion of it relating to the past. She had to tell the rest of it, the part affecting her entire present and future.

"I was very young when I developed the sentiments. *Too* young. Too unworldly. But even so ..." She bit her lip, willing her chin to stop trembling. "When the snowstorm trapped me at Rosemead, those feelings all came rushing back. I truly got to know him this time, and I felt things for him not as a girl but as a woman grown. And now ... and now, I wonder if I'm still in love."

"Oh, Em." Phoebe pulled back to observe her with a look of pure sympathy.

Emily shook her head, refusing to let herself cry again but unable to stop the ache that spread around her heart. "It was never supposed to happen like this. It's all wrong. I think he might care for me, too, but I can't, not now ... I don't know ..."

"Emmy." Her father's hand fell upon her chin, coaxing her to turn to him. "Will you tell me why you accepted Lord Coleville's proposal?" There was nothing accusatory in his question. Only mild curiosity accompanied by a gentle expression he reserved for her, Anna, and Phoebe alone.

She pushed down the lump in her throat, trying to find some coherence amidst her whirling thoughts. "Well, because … because he's a respectable match," she said, repeating the words she'd drummed through her head so many times, trying to make them feel right. "I'm confident he will make a courteous husband, along with a worthy ally for you—"

"No," he cut in, the lines around his mouth becoming tight. "Let me dispel you of any false notions this instant. I agree that Coleville is respectable. I'd value his support in Parliament. However, under no circumstances do I want that to be the basis for your marriage. Especially if your instincts are guiding you elsewhere."

The words crashed over her like a wave, both startling and cathartic. Just like that, he'd freed her from the onus of marrying for a social connection. But even so …

"I don't know if I can rely on my instincts," she choked out. "If I can give up something safe for something unknown. Sometimes, I question whether love is real or merely my mind playing tricks on me to create an illusion."

"I understand that it's frightening," Phoebe said, taking hold of her hand again and giving it a reassuring squeeze. "But if you trust your heart, it will not steer you wrong." Her gaze flitted above Emily's head, locking with her husband's, and it was impossible to miss the brightness that lit her eyes. The tiny smile that made her whole face glow. An expression that the normally stern-faced marquess mimicked, because even after a decade of marriage, he and his wife were still clearly enamored.

"I want to have the same happiness the two of you found together," Emily whispered, her heartbeat a deep patter in her chest. "I *want* to find true love."

"You will, sweetheart." Her father broke the gaze with Phoebe and turned his half-smile upon her, clasping her free hand in his. "Because it *is* real, and it's always worth fighting for."

For a few moments, Emily merely kept sitting, surrounded by the care and support of her parents. She let the warmth of their love—both for her and for each other—fill her, while her mind replayed every piece of advice they'd imparted, accompanied by the steady hum of her grandmother's words: *Prescotts do not cower*.

Until finally, she transferred the sleeping cat to her father's lap—eliciting his scoff, although she knew he secretly enjoyed Marigold's company—and rose from the sofa. The sun was sinking low in the frosty sky, and as much as she didn't want to leave the quiet safety of the drawing room, she needed to retire to her bedchamber and request her lady's maid's assistance. Otherwise, she'd never be presentable in time for Christmas dinner.

But first ... "Thank you." She turned to face her parents, brushing the little tufts of fur from her skirt and giving her flushed cheeks another swipe. She undoubtedly looked an absolute fright, and her voice was still rough from the aftereffects of her sobs. Nonetheless, she hoped they could discern the depth of her gratitude.

Phoebe's eyes continued to sparkle, and the subtle grin lingered upon her lips. "Everything is going to work out exactly as it should."

Emily took a long breath, her nose filling with the yuletide fragrances of cloves and fir branches. With another familiar scent that could only be described as *home*. Her mouth twitched—not in a smile, precisely, but in a tiny upward slant.

Because her heart was still so heavy and uncertain, and once the noisy, cheerful bustle of Christmas dinner ended, she was going to have a long and difficult night of contemplating ahead.

Yet beneath all the heaviness, there were also faint twinges resembling hope.

13

"If the weather is fit after the wedding, I thought we could journey to my property in Yorkshire," Lord Coleville said the next afternoon as he and Emily strolled arm in arm around the wintery grounds of Beaumont.

After another day of sunshine, the large snowdrifts had taken a hit, and the footmen and her cousins alike had created a path in the melting snow that led all the way to the other side of the lake.

Hence why she'd slipped away early from helping her parents distribute St. Stephen's Day boxes to the household staff and had suggested to the earl that they take a walk. After a Christmas Day filled with an abundance of food and excitement, her family had become more subdued today, scattering to various parts of the house to engage in tranquil pastimes. Nonetheless, she preferred the idea of an outdoor rendezvous with Lord Coleville, where there was no risk of anyone listening at the door or barreling in unannounced. The lakeside trail would offer the seclusion she desired, granted that no one came along in the sledge. It would be the perfect place to hold a private and difficult conversation. If she felt so inclined.

"I realize it's not ideal," he continued as they languidly followed the curve in the path, "but I've received word that the manor requires repairs, and there are a few things I'd like to see to myself, if possible."

He's so good, she reflected as he briefly relayed some difficulties with the estate. *So responsible and dedicated, even though he's merely a cousin of the former earl and never expected to inherit.*

He was trying to do his best, and she admired him for it. Except then, for perhaps the thousandth time that day, her thoughts flashed to Nate.

Nate, whose St. Stephen's Day party would commence shortly, after all the hours he'd spent attempting to make every detail just right.

Upon learning of the difficulties Nate experienced with both his ill kitchen maid and his injured hand, her father had sent three kitchen maids, along with four able-bodied footmen, over to Rosemead to assist with the party. As none of them had yet returned, Nate must have gotten over his reluctance and accepted their aid. Regardless, Emily couldn't help wondering how he fared. Were the decorations all in place? Was the food all prepared? Did he survey the great hall and recognize his accomplishments, his worthiness?

And ... when he looked upon the kissing bough above the door, did he think of her?

"I understand, of course, if you'd prefer to go on honeymoon somewhere warmer first," Lord Coleville said, his breath creating a puff of white in the frosty air. "Perhaps we could voyage to the south of France, or Italy—"

No. What he suggested sounded lovely—for another woman. A wife who yearned to travel and could give him the affection he deserved.

However, everything she desired was here in Kent. *Next door.* Perhaps Lord Coleville was a safer choice, but that wasn't where her heart lay. She'd known all along, deep down, that it never would, and it was so unfair to him that she kept pretending. He warranted better than her dishonesty, and she had to tell the truth, as difficult as it would be to find the words to explain how dreadfully she'd erred—

"But I don't believe you wish for any of those things," he concluded, catching her off guard. "Or for a wedding. Not with me."

Her feet abruptly halted on the path, and she spun to face him, the air rushing from her lungs. She blinked several times, taking him in, trying to be certain she'd correctly interpreted his words. There was no anger on his face or malice in his tone. Only a mild look of comprehension that left no doubt regarding his abilities to sense her secret thoughts.

She forced herself to take a breath, her chest tightening with regret. "I'm so sorry. I've gone about everything all wrong. I—"

"May I make a confession, Lady Emily?" His sudden words made her freeze again, and she continued to peer at him a moment before finding the wherewithal to nod.

"My inheriting the earldom in the spring came as a shock," he said. "There's been a great deal to learn, and I want nothing more than to fulfill the responsibilities cast upon me and to prove myself deserving of the title. I took to familiarizing myself with estate management and parliamentary happenings well enough. But then, there was the matter of society. Specifically, of an earl's responsibility to find a suitable wife."

She felt her eyes widen a touch as the meaning of what he implied began to unfold.

"Not that I don't admire you or value the time we spent in each other's company," he rushed to add. "Because I do, most ardently. But ever since issuing the proposal, I haven't been able to stop wondering if my desire to do things right as the earl has perhaps made me a touch hasty. And as for marriage between us ... maybe I recognize the hesitance in you because it exists in me, too."

She waited a moment, letting everything he'd said finish sinking in. And then, her entire body loosened, as if she'd been struck by another clarifying wave.

"I apologize—" he began, but she waved it away with a flick of her wrist, a smile tugging at the corners of her lips.

"I admit, I'm relieved," she said, and when his brows rose, her smile became an airy laugh. "It feels somewhat nice to know I'm not the only one who blundered."

"Oh, Lady Emily." He let out a lengthy sigh, although it ended in a small smile of his own. "If only we'd been wise enough to reach this conclusion *before* I proposed in front of an audience. I don't want our parting to cause any trouble for you."

She shook her head, feeling lighter than she had in a long time. "You needn't worry. It was only my family, and the Prescotts have been the subject of so much ton gossip that they would never purposefully bring another scandal to our door. No one will utter a word about our short-lived betrothal, I'm certain. Indeed, they only want what's best for me. For *us*. For they—and I—admire you as well, and I hope we may all continue calling you a family friend."

"I'd like that," he said. "I could use all the friends I can get as I navigate the labyrinth that is high society."

"It will become easier, I assure you." She set a hand upon his coat sleeve. "You'll adjust to all the intricacies of the ton given time. And somewhere along the way, I imagine you'll find a future countess who *doesn't* make you hesitate and who, in turn, is deserving of your love."

"I thank you, Lady Emily. I hope you're correct." He gave the hand upon his sleeve a fond pat—the parting handshake of friends—and in a silent agreement, they turned, starting back toward the house. "And I hope that you, too, find the love of which you speak."

She trudged along the path, her boots crunching lightly against the thin layer of snow. "Yes, I hope so." The faint warmth of the winter sunrays shone down on her, and she took a breath of the crisp, bracing air. Then released an exhale, followed by the truth. "I rather wonder if I already have."

Her voice was only a murmur, but enough to turn Lord Coleville's head and elicit a wry grin. "Ah. I suspected as much."

The steady rhythm of her footsteps faltered for a beat. "You did?"

"Not all along. Certainly not in any of the London ballrooms," he assured her, putting to rest her sudden fear that she'd made her affections as awkwardly obvious as when she'd been a girl of thirteen. "But yesterday morning, the way Pembrook stared at you as he bid you farewell. I told myself I'd imagined it, but looking back, I'm not certain why I believed my own falsehood. For I could have cut the pining in that room with a knife."

Her lips parted, allowing a gasp to fly out. A gasp, followed by a burst of laughter at how ridiculous that sounded. At how *wonderful* it sounded.

A tingle grabbed hold of her belly, fluttering like the wings of a butterfly. Did Nate truly long for her the way Lord Coleville claimed? She supposed she had reason to believe he did. She *hoped* he did.

But that didn't stop the little trickle of doubt from creeping in. Because what if she'd been wrong yet again? What if, in the end, he could never view her as a wife but only as the immature girl next door?

She forced her feet to keep going, drawing her closer and closer to the back doors of Beaumont Manor. The doors that would lead her through familiar corridors and straight up to her bedchamber, where she could safely remain until morning with some feigned illness, just like on so many Christmases past. Long enough that the party at Rosemead—and its implicit promise for second chances—would be over.

She *could* do that. Or, she could take a chance. She could remain in her bedchamber just long enough to change her dress and put a ribbon in her hair, after which she would get in the sleigh and have it take her back to Rosemead.

Because while the prospect of rejection was terrifying, a risk could yield the greatest reward.

Prescotts do not cower.

She made her footsteps a little quicker, keeping her shoulders held high and her gaze focused straight ahead. On the future.

Off to Rosemead it was.

14

The party was well underway and, by all accounts, a surprising success.

Nate took in what he could of his surroundings, gaining blurred glimpses of the crowded great hall as he spun about in a country dance. Not a pastime in which he'd intended to engage, but his land agent's wife, Mrs. Hammond, had pulled him onto the dance floor and insisted. And while years without practice caused him to shuffle as though he had two left feet, it didn't seem to matter. The dance had none of the practiced finesse one was apt to find in a London ballroom, but the disordered flurry of steps and twirling bodies were accompanied by peals of laughter that knew no comparison.

Everywhere he looked—from the dance floor, to the side tables where guests continued to pick at sweetmeats, to the chairs where those who'd decided not to dance were engaged in animated conversation—there was joy. The same joy he'd witnessed as a child when his mother and father had acted as the party's hosts. Perhaps there'd been a slight decrease in the number of roasted vegetable dishes upon the table when they'd all sat down to dinner. Perhaps the great hall contained a few less ribbons upon the holly boughs than in years past. Be that as it may, the merriment in the room seemed to push against the walls and soar to the towering ceiling.

Because he'd done it. He'd returned to England with the harebrained idea that he could plan a St. Stephen's Day party in a near-vacant house in a matter of days, and he'd succeeded. He hadn't let his tenants down. For once, he hadn't let his father down.

And yet, his own joy stopped just below the surface. It tugged at him faintly, creating small pangs of warmth, but it couldn't reach deep within his chest.

Because *she* wasn't here. Because this was the room where he'd watched her walk away on the arm of her *almost* betrothed—her true betrothed now? The room where ice had formed between his ribs because he knew he'd missed his chance, that she was no longer for him, and even so, the selfish part of him had battled to reemerge and claim her for his own.

Truth be told, it still did, sinking in its angry claws and demanding he fight to get her back.

Even though she'd already chosen a different path.

He missed the next step in the dance entirely, using the moment to suck air into his taut lungs and regather himself. That's when he caught a glimpse of dark hair threaded with a gold ribbon, and every one of his nerve endings jumped to alertness.

Mrs. Hammond tugged on his hand, leading him back into the rhythm of the dance with a wide grin, and he spun as required, the movement jerky. However, his eyes fought to refocus on that spot in the crowd. No, there was nothing remarkable about dark hair and ribbons; any number of his guests possessed both. There was something about that particular figure, though. That flash of features.

He found it again, just a peek before someone taller in stature walked in front of her, and the dance required him to execute another turn. Yet the image had become a little clearer, enough for him to discern a rosebud mouth. A set of gently slanted black brows above eyes the color of rich brandy.

He whirled as if the sight had made him foxed, releasing Mrs. Hammond's hand. Staggering a step to the side. And then, for one perfect, unimpeded moment, he saw her. *Emily.* She stood amidst the throng like a beacon, the light from the sconces seeming to fall upon her alone. The dark green of her gown accentuating her pale skin and hugging every curve. His winter fairytale queen.

Why was she here? Had she come alone? Did that mean ... His heart slammed against the wall of his chest, daring to anticipate.

"Excuse me," he muttered to Mrs. Hammond, who'd already fallen upon another man's arm to finish the dance. He extricated himself from the cluster of revelers, moving toward the side of the room.

Except suddenly, Emily was also moving but in the other direction, weaving amongst the mass of guests until he nearly lost sight of her again.

Where was she going? Had she noticed him? He had to speak to her, had to get to her side at once—

No. He needed to do even better than that.

He needed to give her the recognition she deserved.

Fortunately, one of the violinists glanced up at the opportune moment, and after a single gesture from Nate, the music faded away.

He wasted no time in rushing to the side table, halting just long enough to retrieve the cup of wassail he'd set down and give it a few loud taps with a spoon. Then, he bolted forward, the crowd obligingly parting for him, until he stood before the main doors. Facing the entire jovial scene.

"If I could have your attention." He called out to the merrymakers in a commanding voice he didn't think he'd ever had cause to use before. *A voice befitting a viscount.* "Forgive the interruption, but I'd like to offer a toast."

A low hum followed, in which the guests wound down their conversations and fetched their glasses, and he used the time to quickly scan the room. For his eyes to travel over the sea of people until they connected with the gold ribbon and ebony wisps of hair.

He breathed a sigh of relief. She'd stopped near the side table, where his footman, Daniel, nudged his way in to pass her a glass of wassail. An action for which Nate would have to thank him later.

But first things first—for Emily was here, listening, and he didn't have a second to waste.

He cleared his throat and held his glass up, bringing his gaze back over the eager crowd. "First, I toast to all of you for your loyalty to Rosemead, without which the estate could never prosper. May your Christmastide be plentiful and merry, and may you experience health and happiness in the coming year."

A low cheer began rumbling through the crowd, but he held up his hand, signaling another minute of quiet. "I'd also like to take a moment to toast to my father, Lord Pembrook. I don't think I'm alone in missing his presence at this year's celebration, but I keep his acumen and dedication in mind, and I aspire to follow his example while I oversee the estate in his absence."

He allowed the cheer to build this time, taking the opportunity to catch his breath. To quickly determine the next words he would say, because they needed to be just right. For all he knew, Emily was still a betrothed woman, and her reason for being here had nothing to do with what he hoped. Nonetheless, he at least had to let her know ...

He nudged his glass upward, taking one last look at the array of faces before setting his eyes solely on her. "And last, but certainly not least, I offer a toast and my utmost gratitude to the woman who made this night possible: Lady Emily Prescott."

His audience shuffled, some standing on tiptoe and others craning their necks so they could observe the lady to whom he gestured. As for Emily, he could detect, by the little jolt of her chest, the moment she sucked in a breath. He could see, beneath the candlelight, the hint of pink that spread over her cheeks.

"Some of you may recognize Lady Emily from Beaumont Manor," he said, peering across the space and into those amber eyes. Experiencing a twinge near his heart. "The Prescott family have been neighbors and friends to us here at Rosemead for my entire life. However, Lady Emily went above and beyond the bounds of friendship with her willingness to step in and assist this week. For when I despaired that the poor weather—and other assorted difficulties—would impede this party's success, she was there to prove me wrong. You see, she has twice as many uninjured hands as I and ten times more sense."

A few hearty chuckles spread through the room, and the sight of her lips twitching upward caused his own to respond in kind.

"Her ability to recognize a challenge and confront it without hesitation is unparalleled," he continued. "She turned things I thought impossible into realities. She led with maturity, wisdom, and grace. And she didn't abandon the venture of helping me when I failed to display any of those characteristics."

More laughter ensued, and he couldn't help but join in. He'd been such an oblivious fool in so many ways. Yet Emily had been there the whole time, always knowing what to do. What he needed.

"My household and I agree," he said, his voice suddenly

sobering. His heart racing out of control. "We couldn't have accomplished everything we did, and I could have never fulfilled my vow to uphold the tradition of hosting this party, if not for her. For that, she will have my eternal gratitude and most fervent admiration."

And that only brushes the surface of what I feel for her.

He swallowed down the thick lump of emotion that threatened to make his words break, holding his glass up high. "And so, let's drink. To all of you. To the viscount. And to Lady Emily Prescott."

The great hall erupted with the sounds of appreciative shouts and glasses clinking, and he took a sip of wassail, letting the spiced liquid flow over his tongue. However, out of the myriad things that flooded his senses, he only had eyes for one. *Emily.*

Emily, who raised her glass to him and pressed the wassail to her rosy lips.

Emily, whose eyes shone and dark eyelashes fluttered as those surrounding her showered her with praise.

Emily, who was moving again, the mass of people falling away to give her a path to the front of the room. To him.

She drew nearer, step by ethereal step, until she was at his side, even more breathtakingly beautiful up close. An image he may not be able to paint, but that he knew, beyond a doubt, would stay imprinted in his memory for the rest of his life.

As if by magic, a hush fell over the crowd, until the only sound to reach his ears was the quiet treble of her voice. "Nate." She tilted her chin upward, her eyes rising to the top of the doorframe. "You're standing under the kissing bough."

Oh. So he was. He hadn't considered it before. Hadn't been able to think of anything but the woman in front of him and giving her the words she deserved.

And suddenly, he could think of nothing at all, beyond

the fact that her lips were upon his, and the silence gave way to uproarious applause.

He pulled her against him at once, savoring every second. Her mouth was warm and pliant, sweet and delicately spiced—

And gone from his far too soon, lest their display grow scandalous. However, the way she clasped his hands within hers helped make up for it. The way she turned her amber eyes upon him, and although they contained a sheen—almost as if from tears—he could detect nothing but joy. *The future.*

"Dance with me, Nate." She smiled, giving his left hand a gentle tug, for the violins had restarted, filling the room with a cheery tune.

There was nothing in the world he wanted to do more.

He ambled with her back to the dance floor, his head spinning with wassail and soft lips and hope. It occurred to him, for a flicker of a moment, that he should perhaps warn her he was sorely out of practice when it came to country dances.

Except the instant they fell into the line of couples, the exact steps became meaningless. Instead, they whirled and stumbled and laughed with abandon until the whole world spun, and he felt like he was walking on air. They joined in dance after dance until, little by little, the crowd of revelers surrounding them thinned. Until the time came to relocate to the doorway and bid farewell and Happy Christmas to the tenant families, who began to depart with their gift baskets in hand. Until the last guest was gone, and he instructed his newly returned servants that setting the great hall back in order could wait until tomorrow and that they were to take the rest of the evening to themselves.

Until, finally, he and Emily were well and truly alone.

He hadn't known—hadn't dreamed—this moment would exist. Perhaps that was why he found himself momentarily speechless, capable of nothing but peering at her bright eyes, her flushed cheeks. Of brushing his finger over the silky strand that had escaped from her coiffure.

Perhaps that was why his voice, when it did come, was a rasp, and he found himself stating the obvious, as if to remind himself it was true. "You came back."

She smiled at him, as brilliant as the day's sunlight that had made the snow glitter. Her palm rose to his chest, her fingers splaying against the spot where his heart thrummed below the surface. "How could I stay away when this is the only place I wanted to be?"

"You didn't ... You aren't ..." He trailed off, loath to speak of other men. Of *almost betrotheds*. Yet before he could let himself wish without inhibition, he needed to hear her confirm the truth.

"No." She shook her head, and although he hadn't explained himself, it was clear she'd deciphered his meaning. For she smiled again. Sank her fingertips more deeply into his waistcoat. "In the end, I had to follow my heart."

Something within him seemed to break free, and he leaned in, pressing his forehead to hers. Pressing his hand over hers, too, so he could detect the beat of his heart, which felt more full than he'd ever known possible. "I'm the most fortunate man on earth that your heart led you here."

"Nate." She whispered his name once more—the sweetest sound—and her eyes drifted upward. Yet again, they were standing under the kissing bough.

Consequently, there was only one thing to do. And when he kissed her this time—in the warm, empty great hall, with nothing in the background to disturb them but the yule log's soft crackle—he didn't need to stop.

15

The allure of Emily's lips was far more potent than brandy. The feel of her soft curves beneath his fingertips could keep Nate inebriated for days. He stroked his tongue over hers, his hands sliding down her back, over her hips, to the perfect globes of her backside. Each caress rendering him hungry for more.

Which made it remarkable, really, that he found the presence of mind—and the strength—to overcome the intensifying passion and break the kiss.

"Emily." He cupped her chin, her name coming out ragged and strained. It was a wonder he could speak at all, given the way he fought to catch his breath and that every inch of his body yearned to claim more of her. "I cannot use the snow as an excuse tonight for failing to return you home."

She, too, had grown breathless, her chest rising and falling rapidly beneath her bodice. But she, too, managed speech, her whispered words creating a tiny burst of warmth that tickled his throat. "You do not need an excuse. Not yet." An extra spurt of color flashed across her cheeks. "I told my stepmother I might not be home until late. She said she would ensure that no alarm bells were triggered by my absence until after midnight."

Oh, the clever, brilliant, *marvelous* woman. Thinking ahead. Anticipating this.

His cock pressed insistently against his trousers, the blood rushing through his veins as if it were fire. The last he'd looked at his watch, the hour had been little past ten. Which meant there was nothing stopping him from dragging her back to the table, lifting her skirts, and running his tongue all over her sex in a way he hadn't stopped thinking about since the first time—

But no. As much as he craved the intimate taste of her and the sound of her desirous cries filling his ears *now*, without delay, this moment called for something more. They may not have all night together, but there was enough time to lay her across his bed and savor her. To show her the depth of every-thing he felt.

He leaned in close to her, allowing the tip of his tongue to brush along her earlobe. "Will you come upstairs with me?"

She nodded against his fingertips, her exhale causing her chest to tremble. Her pupils wide with desire.

He could put the kissing bough to exceptionally good use and claim her lips again then and there, except they would never make it upstairs if that happened. And so, he opted simply to twine his fingers with hers, taking a final cursory glance at the well-used great hall before leading her out of the room and up the stairs, all the way to his bedchamber.

Only then, after he'd shut the door behind them and they were safely enshrouded in the large room with its turned-down counterpane and hearty fire, did he allow himself the pleasure of another deep, impassioned kiss.

He held her tight in his arms and kissed her all the way to the edge of his bed, loving the way she teased him with little flicks of her tongue, the way her fingernails sank into his back as if to claim him.

He kissed her jawline. The pulse point in her throat. Her collarbone. All while his fingers made their way down the row of buttons at her back, freeing each one from its loop, and she set to work as well, deftly unfastening his cravat and moving on to his coat and waistcoat.

Her gown sagged at the same moment she hauled the coat from his shoulders, and they stood before one another, each a little more exposed. Still not nearly enough, though.

He gave her a moment to pull off his waistcoat and help drag the shirt over his head. To press her palms against his bare chest, the soft heat of them sending a jolt of longing straight to his groin.

And then, he could wait no more. He wrenched the laces of her stays, undoing knots until the garment was loose and he could throw it to the floor. Leaving her in only stockings and a shift that was semi-translucent in the firelight, hinting at the perfection he would find underneath it.

"So beautiful," he murmured, taking hold of the ribbon that kept that last bit of fabric in place. Giving it a tug.

The thin cotton pooled to the floor, and suddenly, every part of her was his to revere. The smooth, pale skin. The deep pink nipples. The dark triangle of curls between her legs. "*So beautiful*," he couldn't help repeating, because everything he desired was in front of him, better than he could have possibly imagined. "So exquisite. So perfect."

The best part was, she displayed no hesitation about being bared to him but allowed him to study, to relish. All while giving him an alluring little half-smile that may very well be the death of him.

He lowered her to the bed, kicking off his boots so he could crawl up after her, making a place for himself to kneel between her legs. Then, he brought his head to her breast, taking one of the pert nipples into his mouth and stroking it with his tongue. Pinching the other between his fingertips.

She rewarded him with a breathy cry, her body jerking against the mattress. "Oh, God, Nate, *please*." Her hands began flailing, gripping his hair, his shoulders, moving down his abdomen and toward his fall.

Which was his signal to stretch out his body so he lay against the lower part of the mattress, his lips in the ideal position to drop kisses around her navel. One brush of her fingers against his cock and he'd lose sight of reason entirely, and he couldn't allow that to happen. Not until he felt certain she was prepared for him. That every part of this would be good for her.

Her gasp of surprise turned into another cry as his mouth connected with her sex, his tongue tracing over the folds he'd gotten to know so intimately while kneeling beside the great hall dining table. Somehow, she tasted even sweeter than last time, the essence of her going to his head like he'd drunk the whole bowl of wassail. And somehow, the moan she gave when he began circling her secret bundle of nerves made his body ignite with even more potency than before.

He licked and caressed without relenting, dragging his hand up her thigh. Easing a finger into her entrance, where she was so hot, so wet.

His cock throbbed with appreciation—with *want*—and likewise, her body began to quiver. Her cries to escalate. He kept stroking her with his finger, dragging it in and out in time with the sweeps of his tongue against her clitoris.

Until suddenly, she was pulsing around him, her intimate muscles clenching him tight as she found her release.

He lapped at her flesh, staying with her until the spasms faded, and instead of clutching his hair, she tugged at his shoulders, prompting him to move upward again.

He willingly obliged, kissing the flat surface of her belly, the valley between her breasts, as he went. He'd been no stranger to pleasure-filled nights during his idle years on the Continent, but all those encounters put together couldn't compare to the longing that currently shot through his veins. However, when she reached for his fall again, his hand shot out to capture her wrist, stopping her fingers just inches short from where he most yearned for them to be.

"Nate." Her voice was breathless, and her eyes seemed to grow darker as they took him in. "I want ... I want to know how it feels to have you inside me."

God in heaven. The mere suggestion caused his already aching cock to throb painfully against his trousers. "I desire that, too, more than you could know," he rasped. "But I need you to understand."

He paused, fighting to maintain his final tentative grip on reason, because this was too important not to get right. For this wasn't merely a pleasureful yet meaningless encounter, but so much more. "I don't intend for our coupling to be something we enjoy only for one night, brought on by the merriment of the yuletide season," he said stiffly, his chest pounding with a mixture of sensations he'd never had cause to experience before. "If we do this, I want it to mean forever."

Her kiss-swollen lips parted as she absorbed his words. And then ...

And then, she smiled, that brilliant expression that lit up his world. "I want forever with you, Nate."

Forever.

He leaned down, unable to go another second without sealing the word with a kiss. It would seem his spur-of-the-moment decision to return to England was the best thing he'd done in his life.

His hands ran down the curve of her breasts, taking hold of her waist. Flipping their positions, so all of a sudden, he was the one who rested against the mattress while she lay sprawled out on top of him.

She released a quick huff of breath, pushing herself up to sit astride him, her gaze posing a silent question.

He drew her hand back to his fall, bringing her fingers to hover just above the top buttons. "When my hand has healed," he said, the last word becoming a hiss as she immediately set to work undoing the buttons, "there is no limit to the positions I wish to explore with you. For now, though, we would each be best served if you were to lower yourself onto me."

Her fingers halted for just an instant before understanding flickered in her eyes, and she continued unfastening buttons, the whisper of her touch setting his body aflame. "I know how it's done," she mumbled, releasing the bottom of his fall and freeing his erection. Hauling the trousers from his hips so that he, too, was completely bare. "The Beaumont library has some illustrated books that I don't believe I was supposed to see, but I perused them, nevertheless."

Did she *want* him to expire on the spot? Did she have any idea how damn alluring she was? He grasped her hips, helping her get into position above his rigid cock. "I'm going to need you to provide *far* more details about that."

"There was a page where the woman sat upon the man, just like this. I always thought it looked …" She sank down a touch, her brow furrowing as she absorbed the unfamiliar sensation.

Even that tiny hint of her was enough to send another explosion of sparks shooting through his core, and his hips quivered, frantic with the urge to move.

But he didn't. He used every shred of restraint he possessed to keep himself still as she lowered herself a little more, inch by gratifying inch. She stretched to accommodate him, absorbing him into her tightness, her heat. Until, with a little gasp, she seated herself on him fully, her eyes screwing shut and her forehead puckering from the shock of it.

"Let yourself relax, love." He released her hip, sliding his hand up her stomach and to the slope of her breasts. Brushing over her nipples and trailing back down until he reached the sensitive peak between her legs, giving it a few languid caresses. "You still didn't tell me how you thought the illustration looked."

Her eyes flew open, her body shifting against his, her hips rising. Then falling. Something flashed across her features, almost like a fire had been lit behind her eyes, and she did it again, gliding up his length and plummeting back down. He bit his lip, hard, forcing himself to remain motionless except for the quickening circles his fingers traced against her clitoris.

When she gasped this time, it wasn't a sound of surprised discomfort but of pleasure. "It looked blissful," she moaned, finding an up-and-down rhythm that didn't stop.

He groaned along with her, his own need quickly spiraling out of control. She was like a goddess above him, riding him, driving him higher with each plunge. Driving herself higher, too, for her cries grew more desperate, her movements more rapid.

Finally, he allowed his hips to move, thrusting upward to meet her each time she sank down. And all at once, she shattered, her muscles squeezing not his finger this time but his cock.

It was beyond what he could take. With one last thrust, his body exploded with the force of his release—a violent, consuming pleasure that tore through him until he was left panting and weightless.

With a beguiling grin, she collapsed against him, nestling her head beneath his chin. "It *was* blissful," she said between breaths, her heartbeat creating tiny vibrations upon his chest.

And he smiled as well, because he couldn't agree more. He

held her tight to him, stroking her shoulders and back, murmuring words about how glorious she was, inhaling the scent of her hair. *Rich and warm, like vanilla*, he thought, now that the aromas of greenery and kitchen spices were no longer around to interfere.

If he had one regret about the night, it was that the clock kept moving forward, making it impossible for them to linger.

Yet as unpleasant a chore as it would be to extricate himself from under her body and head out into the cold, only to return to his bed alone, there was no need to grow morose.

For this was only the beginning.

16

E mily found it no easy feat to rise from Nate's bed and prepare for the journey back to Beaumont Manor.

She'd known all along that they didn't have the full night together. That her family would be waiting for her. Regardless, each brush of Nate's fingertips against her skin as he refastened her laces made her very much wish he was undoing them instead. And when they removed themselves to the great hall and he set the cloak upon her shoulders, she couldn't help but long for the relentless snowfall that had kept them confined from the outside world, unaccountable to anyone.

The only thing that sustained her, as they went out into the frosty darkness and Nate helped her into the sleigh, was his fervent promise: "This is the one and only time, I swear, that I'll be bringing you home instead of keeping you in my bed."

He climbed in beside her, and with a flick of the reins, the sleigh began gliding over the moonlit snow, on track to return her to Beaumont just before the stroke of midnight. She nuzzled against him beneath the thick blanket they shared, glancing up at the stars above. How was it they seemed brighter now than when she'd first arrived at Rosemead? That the air had become crisper? That her body was more alive, humming with anticipation?

"I never thought I'd have cause to so fervidly miss the snowstorm," Nate said in echo of her own thoughts as they started toward the woods, the horses' bells jingling merrily in the background. He pressed his fingertips under her chin, gently prodding her to turn to him. "I've realized now how wrong I was to curse it. For I have the snow to thank for guiding you to me."

She'd smiled and laughed more this night than she could ever recall doing on any other in her life, and in keeping with the tendency, her mouth curved upward at his words. "I've reached the conclusion that bringing in greenery early is actually quite lucky."

"Agreed." He grinned back at her, his features bright beneath the glow of the sleigh's lamps. "I've never felt luckier, and I'm grateful, Emily. For all the reasons I cited in my toast, although those are only part of it. They say nothing of my gratitude for the way you've come back into my life as so much more than a neighbor. For the way you've captured my heart."

Her own heart leaped and fluttered in response. He'd spoken of forever right before their bodies joined and he brought her pleasure to new and dizzying heights. She'd begun to dream and hope. However, hearing him admit the depth of his feelings made the possibility feel so much more tangible.

His hand went down to clasp hers, and although the night was cold, an exhilarating warmth spread through her limbs. "I've wasted so many years seeking fulfillment in the wrong places that I don't want to lose another second," he said, squeezing her fingers tight. Peering at her with those eyes of clear, intense gray. "My father needed to travel to obtain his happy ending. Mine, though, has been next door the entire time. I could drag this out by suggesting we arrange for regular carriage rides together, or formal visits in the Beaumont drawing room, or whatever else courting couples are supposed to do. However, none of those things will alter what I already know. I love you. When I envision my life as the future Viscount Pembrook, you're the only woman I can possibly imagine as my future viscountess. I meant what I said: I want forever with you. Will you do me the honor of becoming my wife?"

Her breath stuttered, creating a white wisp in the darkness as her mouth grew slack. She'd chided herself for being young and foolish, for letting her affections land where they weren't warranted. But what if her heart had been correct all along? What if everything she'd once dreamed of, but had long thought impossible, could really come true?

Her mind flashed back to the sketched hearts in her girlhood diary. To all the times she'd pinched her cheeks and practiced her laugh and tied colorful ribbons in her hair.

But mostly, it flashed to him. To the man who'd stubbornly dragged the yule log through the woods because he wished to do right by his father and estate. Who'd tucked a rose behind her ear when she'd been afraid. The man who'd trusted her with his secrets, who'd brought her to his bed, who'd taken everything she thought she knew about both desire and joy and made it a hundred times bigger.

Yes, this was all happening quickly. But like him, she didn't need more time to realize what she wanted from the future. She already knew what she felt deep inside.

And so, she gazed back at him, revealing the truth that had long existed as a suggestion in her heart but had spent the past few days blossoming into something new and profound. Something unbreakable. "I love you, too, Nathaniel Pembrook. I don't need to wait any longer before telling you that yes, I will marry you."

For an instant, there was nothing between them but the

sound of hooves against snow and the tingle of bells. No movement but the flicker of the lanterns and the shadows of trees passing by.

Until suddenly, his lips were upon hers, pulling her into an ardent embrace. Although one that lasted only a moment before the sleigh veered, and her eyes flew open just in time to see him reclaiming his hold on the reins.

He gave her a sheepish grin that rapidly turned wide. Nonsensical, even. A grin she felt assured was mirrored on her own features, for the next thing, her laugh rang out into the night.

He took a minute to tighten the reins around his hand before turning back to her, giving their interrupted kiss a proper, albeit quick, finale. "You've made me so happy, love. I plan to devote the rest of my life to returning the favor."

They spent the remainder of the sleigh ride in much the same way—alternating between stolen kisses and glances ahead to ensure that the sleigh was indeed still heading toward Beaumont Manor.

They kissed as they crossed the border back onto Beaumont land.

They kissed as a few dark, puffy clouds drifted overhead.

They kissed as a breeze rippled through the air, the bitterness no match for the heat of Nate's body and the warmth that filled her from head to toe.

And they kissed as, once again, the sky opened, surrounding them with a dusting of soft, silent snowflakes.

Epilogue

January 25, 1817
Paris, France

Dear Nathaniel,
How does one begin a letter when one's heart is bursting with so
many things that it's difficult to say which should take
precedence?
I suppose I should start in order of events and alert you of the
various commendations that have reached me regarding the St.
Stephen's Day fete at Rosemead. By all accounts, it was as
merry and festive an evening as the house has ever seen, and I
don't think I need to tell you that, given your limited time and
resources to prepare, you accomplished an impressive feat
indeed.
I'm so grateful for the devoted friends and servants we've
amassed over the years who helped make the evening possible.
The Prescott family are as loyal of neighbors as one could ever
hope to find, and I've written to Lord Rockliffe to express my
utmost appreciation to his entire household. As for our own
faithful staff, they are all to be commended for their work, and

I'm pleased to hear that Mrs. White and Mrs. Ruck have both departed for a well-deserved holiday.

But mostly, I'm grateful for you. And while I hope you already know this, I think it still warrants saying: I'm <u>proud</u> of you, my son. I regret the misunderstandings that cloud our past more than I can express, but having you return to me, and seeing you choose to continue back to England and accept what is your birthright, was the greatest gift I could have possibly received. Your dedication to carrying on Rosemead's longstanding yuletide tradition is admirable. Should you use even a fraction of that care and devotion when dealing with other estate matters, Rosemead is sure to thrive for many years to come. Rest assured that whenever you seek guidance, I'm always here to offer it from afar. Yet when the day does come that the title, and everything along with it, falls solely to you, I have no doubt I'll be leaving it in the best of hands.

As for the other news to come out of St. Stephen's Day—namely, your betrothal to Lady Emily Prescott—what can I do but extend my most heartfelt congratulations? I would have hesitated to say this in your younger years—for youth often seem inclined to do the opposite of what's advised by their elders—but I trust you've reached an age where I can safely tell you: I always hoped. I don't wish to sound like a meddling old matchmaker, but there is something about the two of you that I've long believed would suit. Lady Emily is a delightful young woman, and I have every confidence she'll make you an affectionate and steadfast wife. She has already done Rosemead proud with her role in organizing the party, and I can think of no one I'd rather call my daughter and the future viscountess.

My only grievance in all this is that you didn't have a longer betrothal period, for had I known of your intention to marry, I would have been on a ship bound for England at once so I could witness your happy day. Even though you had only a small ceremony in the Beaumont drawing room (and what a way to bring in the new year, might I add), I would have very much liked to be there by your side.

That being said, I cannot fault you for your haste. I know how difficult it is to wait when you love someone to the point that it consumes your entire person, and if life gives you the opportunity to unrestrainedly follow your heart, I'm a strong believer that you should take it.

I <u>have</u> taken that opportunity for myself, at long last, and your support and understanding have helped make my happiness complete. The only thing to augment it further has been knowing you found that same happiness, too—the type of joy that fills your soul and wraps around your heart because you know those crucial pieces of yourself are kept safe in the hands of another.

I wish you both many blissful and prosperous years together, and a love that flourishes with each passing day. I was so delighted to hear that you're considering a wedding trip to France come spring; please know that Henry and I would welcome you and your new bride with open arms.

Until then, I remain

Your loving father

~

THE END

Bonus Content

Sign up for Jane's newsletter to get access to free bonus content, including a steamy second epilogue for *His Christmas Rose*. You will also be the first to know about special promotions and new releases, including what's coming next in the Rockliffe Dynasty series. Join now at: www.janemaguireauthor.com/newsletter

About the Author

Jane Maguire is a Canadian author whose lifelong passions for history, writing, and love stories inevitably led her to begin penning historical romance novels. While her love of historical fiction spans all eras, she focuses her writing on high society in the regency period. She enjoys crafting stories with lots of angst, which makes giving her characters their happily ever afters all the more satisfying.

When she isn't at her computer writing and researching, you can find her vacationing in the Rocky Mountains, playing classical music on the piano, or simply curling up with a cup of tea and a good book. She lives with her husband, two kids, and a very floofy cat.

You can find Jane online at www.janemaguireauthor.com.